**READ & LISTEN** OS MELHORES CONTOS DO SÉCULO XX EM VERSÃO ORIGINAL NA ÍNTEGRA

*"Sometimes all we need is a fine, short story."*

# Roald Dahl
*Parson's Pleasure*

•

# Edith Wharton
*The Other Two*

*"With the inventive power of a Thomas Edison and the imagination of a Lewis Carroll... Roald Dahl is a wizard of comedy and grotesque, an artist with a marvelously topsy-turvy[1] sense of the ridiculous in life."*
Cleveland Plain Dealer

•

*"Few can equal Wharton in getting under the skin of a character or in getting under the skin of a reader. And in purity of style Mrs Wharton is still unsurpassed."*
The New York Times

---

1 **topsy-turvy:** louco, extravagante (literalmente, de ponta-cabeça)

© 1959 por Roald Dahl Nominee Limited. Permissão de
Edith Whaton Estate e Watkins/Loomis Agency.
© 2011 Martins Editora Livraria Ltda.,
São Paulo, para a presente edição.

| | |
|---:|:---|
| **Publisher** | *Evandro Mendonça Martins Fontes* |
| **Coordenação editorial** | *Anna Dantes* |
| **Produção editorial** | *Alyne Azuma* |
| **Tradução** | *Betty Pinto de Nisembaum* |
| **Revisão** | *Denise Roberti Camargo* |
| | *André Albert* |
| | *Dinarte Zorzanelli da Silva* |
| **Biografias e apresentações** | *Laura Fernández* |
| **Locução de "Parson´s Pleasure"** | *Julian Jahanpour* |
| **Locução de "The Other Two"** | *Amber Ockrassa* |
| **Gravação** | *RecLab* |
| **Técnico** | *Francesc Gosalves* |

**Dados Internacionais de Catalogação na Publicação (CIP)
(Câmara Brasileira do Livro, SP, Brasil)**

Dahl, Roald, 1916-1990.
 Parson's pleasure / Roald Dahl. The other two / Edith
Wharton / [tradução Betty Pinto de Nisembaum]. – 1. ed. – São
Paulo : Martins Martins Fontes, 2011.

 Título original: Parson's pleasure ; The other two.
 Inclui CD.
 ISBN 978-85-8063-007-7

 1. Contos ingleses 2. Contos norte-americanos I. Wharton,
Edith, 1862-1937. II. Título. III. Título: The other two.

| | |
|:---|---:|
| 11-02231 | CDD-823.91 |
| | -813 |

**Índices para catálogo sistemático:**
1. Contos : Literatura inglesa 823.91
2. Contos : Literatura norte-americana 813

*Todos os direitos desta edição para o Brasil reservados à*
***Martins Editora Livraria Ltda.***
*Av. Dr. Arnaldo, 2076*
*01255-000 São Paulo SP Brasil*
*Tel. (11) 3116.0000*
*info@martinseditora.com.br*
*www.martinsmartinsfontes.com.br*

SUMÁRIO

INTRODUÇÃO.................................................................................................... 11

# Roald Dahl
BIOGRAFIA......................................................................................................... 15
APRESENTAÇÃO DO CONTO....................................................................... 17
*Parson's Pleasure*............................................................................................ 19

# Edith Wharton
BIOGRAFIA......................................................................................................... 65
APRESENTAÇÃO DO CONTO....................................................................... 67
*The Other Two*................................................................................................ 69

INTRODUÇÃO
## Dê um passo além e leia os clássicos em versão original

Para muitos de nós, ler em versão original supõe um desafio por vezes irrealizável. Habituados a nossa própria língua, ficamos frustrados quando não entendemos todas as palavras de um texto. Quantas vezes deixamos um livro de lado porque não queremos consultar o dicionário a toda hora? Essa consulta (quase sempre obrigatória) se soma ao desconhecimento das referências culturais, à dificuldade de perceber os matizes, a ironia do autor etc. Logo nos aborrecemos por não conseguir compreender a essência do relato e acabamos fechando o livro e buscando a versão traduzida.

Na coleção READ & LISTEN a leitura e audição do texto original produzem experiências tão únicas quanto a de contemplar uma pintura em vez de sua reprodução. Não só se aprende como também se desfruta e assimila o verdadeiro espírito do relato.

Aqui, os leitores podem ter acesso aos melhores contos dos mais respeitados autores de língua inglesa, com as ferramentas necessárias para compreender os textos em sua totalidade.

Foi-se o tempo de ler com o dicionário do lado. Cada conto inclui um extenso glossário para que não seja necessário interromper a leitura. Além de todas as palavras que você pode não entender, ele apresenta referências culturais, deixa claras as nuances e permite compreender todos os toques irônicos de cada conto. Para quem quer praticar a compreensão oral ou simplesmente ouvir o texto enquanto o lê, nada mais simples. Ponha o CD com a versão em áudio dos contos para tocar, sente-se, relaxe e deixe que um locutor nativo conte a história. Porque não há maneira melhor de colocar ao seu alcance essas obras-primas do que rompendo as barreiras que o mantiveram longe delas durante tanto tempo.

Quem tem medo dos clássicos?

E por falar em clássicos... Nossa seleção se guiou por várias premissas: em primeiro lugar, os contos tinham de ser sugestivos e não muito complexos; em segundo lugar, tinham de representar o mundo próprio de cada autor. Clássicos em miniatura, inesquecíveis, os contos desta coleção devem ser lidos com cuidado, degustando cada frase, cada palavra. São obras capazes de transformar seus personagens em alguém conhecido, quase familiar, que poderia ser seu melhor amigo.

Acreditamos que, depois de tanto tempo aprendendo inglês, chegou seu momento de desfrutar. Você merece.

# Roald Dahl

*Parson's Pleasure*

*"That was a bloody good carpenter put this job together and I don't care what the parson says."*

BIOGRAFIA
**Roald Dahl**

Roald Dahl (Llandaf, País de Gales, 1916 – Oxford, Inglaterra, 1990) sempre foi um homem alto demais. E um homem de sorte. Ao completar 26 anos, já tinha sobrevivido a dois acidentes aéreos e uma emboscada em terra (teve de se fingir de morto para não ser metralhado). Com apenas sete horas de voo, tornou-se o soldado que melhor pilotava na sua divisão (nos idos de 1939, quando estourou a Segunda Guerra Mundial).

Não escreveu nada até ser mandado de volta para casa em 1942, mas já tinha lido muito, principalmente histórias de monstros. Sua história favorita quando criança era "Trolls", de Jonas Lie, e também tinha escutado sua mãe contar tenebrosos contos noruegueses. Chegou a confessar em uma ocasião que, se não fossem as histórias que sua mãe contava todas as noites, talvez não tivesse se tornado escritor.

Roald, a quem chamaram assim por causa do explorador Roald Amundsen (herói nacional norueguês que se atreveu a conquistar o Polo Norte), teve uma infância complicada. Após a morte trágica do seu pai (duas semanas depois da morte de uma de suas irmãs por causa de uma apendicite) quando tinha apenas três anos, sua mãe hesitou entre voltar para sua Noruega natal ou continuar na Inglaterra, mas acabou ficando no Reino Unido, porque o desejo de seu marido era que seus filhos fossem criados em colégios privados britânicos. Para isso Sophie teve de mandar os filhos para um internato, no qual Roald passou por muitas dificuldades.

Ele escrevia uma carta diariamente para sua mãe e tornou-se o rei das travessuras (a mais famosa foi quando convenceu alguns companheiros a colocar um rato morto em um pote de guloseimas da loja de doces do povoado). No ensino médio, logo se tornou um dos meninos mais populares.

Quando terminou os estudos, trabalhou para a companhia Shell na Tanzânia, onde viveu como um autêntico marajá. Com pouco mais de 20 anos tinha cozinheiro e empregados. Mas então explodiu a Segunda Guerra Mundial, e Dahl se tornou o piloto mais sortudo da sua divisão.

Superados o acidente que o deixou cego por um tempo (enquanto se recuperava, no Hospital de Alexandria, se apaixonou por uma enfermeira, caso que não deu em nada), e a posterior emboscada em terra na qual quase perdeu a vida, ele foi mandado aos Estados Unidos. Lá atuou como agente secreto para a CIA britânica junto ao criador de James Bond, Ian Flemming.

Foi lá que escreveu e publicou seu primeiro conto, "A Piece of Cake", a história do acidente aéreo que quase lhe custou a vida e foi publicado no *The Saturday Evening Post*. Dahl tinha 26 anos.

Em seguida vieram quase uma centena de histórias para adultos (recompiladas em 19 volumes, dentre os quais se destacam *Tales of the Unexpected* e *Beijo*, onde aparece o conto incluído nesta edição) e aproximadamente vinte histórias para crianças, que povoaram os sonhos e pesadelos das crianças do século XX (*Os Gremlins*, *A fantástica fábrica de chocolate*, *James e o pêssego gigante*, *As Bruxas* e *Matilda*, entre outras).

Casou-se com a atriz Patricia Neal aos 37 anos. Tiveram cinco filhos. Divorciaram-se após 30 anos de casamento porque o escritor teve um caso com a melhor amiga dela, vinte anos mais jovem que ele. Sete anos depois, em 1990, Roald Dahl faleceu (aos 74 anos) e foi enterrado entre chocolates, após um comovente funeral viking.

LAURA FERNÁNDEZ

APRESENTAÇÃO DO CONTO
**Parson's Pleasure**

Cyril Boggis tem um segredo. Cyril Boggis vende móveis velhos e está ficando rico. Por quê? Eis o segredo dele. Uma manhã de domingo, ele foi visitar sua mãe, que vive isolada em um casarão no campo na Inglaterra. No caminho, teve um problema com o carro e, assim como no clássico de Alfred Hitchcock, mas trocando o motel sórdido por um casarão cheio de agricultores, teve de pedir ajuda (um telefonema) para a dona de uma mansão do povoado. O que aconteceu ali? Ele descobriu algumas cadeiras antigas de valor incalculável. E o que Cyril fez? Barganhou até o indizível com a senhora e conseguiu levar as cadeiras para casa e vendê-las a um preço muito superior ao da compra. Sendo assim, agora, todo domingo, Boggis se dedica a percorrer o campo de carro até descobrir um novo casarão isolado. E o que faz? Finge ter um problema com o carro e pede um telefone? Não, algo muito melhor. Manda fazer centenas de cartões de visita nos quais se lê "Cyril Boggis: Reverendo e Presidente da Sociedade para Conservação de Móveis Raros". E a coisa funciona bem? Sim, até que se depara com os três brutos proprietários de uma majestosa cômoda do século XV e quase perde a cabeça.

Considerado um dos seus melhores contos e incluído em *Beijo*, sua quarta antologia de narrativas, editada em 1960, "Parson's Pleasure" é uma dessas histórias criativas, engenhosas, que Dahl sempre manejou tão bem, com um final totalmente inusitado e, claro, o delicioso humor negro e o retrato de costumes absurdo do autor. Porque Dahl não foi só um grande escritor infantil (não se pode esquecer que ele é o criador dos temidos Gremlins e do astuto Willy Wonka e sua fábrica de chocolate); suas histórias para adultos (sempre com a famosa e inesperada virada final) marcaram um antes e um depois no que se refere à literatura satírica. Ele escreveu dois romances (*Some Time Never: A Fable for Supermen* e *My Uncle Oswald*), que passaram despercebidos diante da avalanche de formidáveis pequenos universos que podia construir em apenas 20 páginas. O caso que nos ocupa é um bom exemplo do que Dahl sabia fazer de melhor: converter um sonho em pesadelo (e nesse ponto deveríamos voltar ao assunto Gremlins: o que parece ser um bicho de pelúcia carinhoso pode acabar se tornando um sinistro monstro verde.)

Simples e ameno, o estilo de Roald Dahl é quase infantil. A única virada inesperada é dada pela própria trama. As frases se desenvolvem sem cortes e permitem uma leitura fluida e sem muitas complicações lexicais. Todas as dúvidas de vocabulário podem ser solucionadas consultando o glossário que aparece em cada página do conto. E ainda por cima, a versão gravada da história nos permite desfrutar ainda mais daquilo que sem dúvida é um delirante conto de fadas para adultos. Bem-vindos ao apaixonante universo de Roald Dahl. Aproveitem!

LAURA FERNÁNDEZ

*Parson's Pleasure*

Mr. Boggis was driving the car slowly, leaning back[1] comfortably in the seat with one elbow resting on the sill[2] of the open window. How beautiful the countryside, he thought; how pleasant to see a sign or two of summer once again. The primroses[3] especially. And the hawthorn[4]. The hawthorn was exploding white and pink and red along the hedges[5] and the primroses were growing underneath in little clumps[6], and it was beautiful.

He took one hand off the wheel[7] and lit himself a cigarette. The best thing now, he told himself, would be to make for the top of Brill Hill. He could see it about half a mile ahead. And that must be the village of Brill, that cluster[8] of cottages among the trees right on the very summit[9]. Excellent. Not many of his Sunday sections had a nice elevation like that to work from.

He drove up the hill and stopped the car just short of the summit[10] on the outskirts[11] of the village. Then he got out and looked around. Down below, the countryside was spread out before him[12] like a huge green carpet. He could see for

---

1 **leaning back:** inclinado; apoiado • 2 **sill:** peitoril • 3 **primroses:** prímulas • 4 **hawthorn:** espinheiro • 5 **hedges:** cercas vivas • 6 **clumps:** moitas • 7 **wheel:** volante • 8 **cluster:** aglomerado; grupo • 9 **the very summit:** lá no topo • 10 **just short of the summit:** bem à beira da colina • 11 **outskirts:** limites • 12 **spread out before him:** se estendia na frente dele

miles. It was perfect. He took a pad[1] and pencil from his pocket, leaned against the back of the car, and allowed his practised eye[2] to travel slowly over the landscape.

He could see one medium farmhouse over on the right, back in the fields, with a track[3] leading to it from the road. There was another larger one beyond it. There was a house surrounded by tall elms[4] that looked as though it might be a Queen Anne[5], and there were two likely farms[6] away over on the left. Five places in all. That was about the lot[7] in this direction.

Mr. Boggis drew a rough sketch[8] on his pad showing the position of each so that he'd be able to find them easily when he was down below, then he got back into the car and drove up through the village to the other side of the hill. From there he spotted[9] six more possibles—five farms and one big white Georgian house. He studied the Georgian[10] house through his binoculars. It had a clean prosperous look, and the garden was well ordered. That was a pity. He ruled it out[11] immediately. There was no point in calling on the prosperous[12].

In this square then, in this section, there were ten possibles in all. Ten was a nice number, Mr. Boggis told himself.

---

1 **pad:** bloco • 2 **his practised eye:** seu olho experiente • 3 **a track:** um caminho • 4 **elms:** olmos • 5 **Queen Anne:** estilo arquitetônico do princípio do século XVIII (refere-se ao estilo da casa.) • 6 **two likely farms:** provavelmente duas fazendas • 7 **that was about the lot:** era praticamente tudo • 8 **a rough sketch:** um croqui; rascunho • 9 **he spotted:** ele localizou • 10 **Georgian:** estilo arquitetônico muito refinado dos séculos XVIII e XIX • 11 **he ruled it out:** ele descartou; excluiu • 12 **there was no point in calling on the prosperous:** não fazia sentido fazer uma visita aos afortunados

Just the right amount for a leisurely[1] afternoon's work. What time was it now? Twelve o'clock. He would have liked a pint of beer in the pub before he started, but on Sundays they didn't open until one. Very well, he would have it later. He glanced[2] at the notes on his pad. He decided to take the Queen Anne first, the house with the elms. It had looked nicely dilapidated[3] through the binoculars. The people there could probably do with some money[4]. He was always lucky with Queen Annes, anyway. Mr. Boggis climbed back into the car, released the handbrake[5], and began cruising[6] slowly down the hill without the engine[7].

Apart from the fact that he was at this moment disguised[8] in the uniform of a clergyman[9], there was nothing very sinister about Mr. Cyril Boggis. By trade he was a dealer in antique furniture[10], with his own shop and showroom in the King's Road, Chelsea. His premises[11] were not large, and generally he didn't do a great deal of business, but because he always bought cheap, very very cheap, and sold very very dear[12], he managed to make quite a tidy little income[13] every year. He was a talented salesman[14], and when buying or selling a piece he could slide[15] smoothly into whichever mood[16]

---

1 **leisurely:** vagarosa • 2 **he glanced:** ele olhou de relance • 3 **dilapidated:** deteriorada • 4 **could probably do with some money:** provavelmente precisavam de dinheiro • 5 **released the handbrake:** soltou o freio de mão • 6 **began cruising:** começou a dirigir-se • 7 **without the engine:** com o motor desligado • 8 **disguised:** disfarçado • 9 **clergyman:** clérigo • 10 **by trade he was a dealer in antique furniture:** se dedicava ao comércio de móveis antigos • 11 **premises:** seu local • 12 **dear:** caro • 13 **quite a tidy little income:** uma considerável renda • 14 **salesman:** vendedor • 15 **he could slide:** ele podia transitar • 16 **mood:** humor; atitude

suited the client best. He could become grave and charming[1] for the aged[2], obsequious[3] for the rich, sober[4] for the godly[5], masterful[6] for the weak, mischievous[7] for the widow, arch and saucy for the spinster[8]. He was well aware of his gift[9], using it shamelessly[10] on every possible occasion; and often, at the end of an unusually good performance, it was as much as he could do to prevent himself[11] from turning aside and taking a bow[12] or two as the thundering[13] applause of the audience went rolling through[14] the theatre.

In spite of this rather clownish quality[15] of his, Mr. Boggis was not a fool. In fact it was said of him[16] by some that he probably knew as much about French, English and Italian furniture as anyone else in London. He also had surprisingly good taste[17], and he was quick to recognize and reject[18] an ungraceful[19] design, however genuine the article might be. His real love, naturally, was for the work of the great eighteenth-century English designers, Ince, Mayhew, Chippendale, Robert Adam, Manwaring, Inigo Jones, Hepplewhite, Kent, Johnson, George Smith, Lock, Sheraton, and the rest of them, but even with these he occasionally drew the line[20]. He refused, for example, to allow a single piece

---

1 **grave and charming:** sério e encantador • 2 **the aged:** os mais idosos • 3 **obsequious:** servil • 4 **sober:** sóbrio; solene • 5 **the godly:** religiosos; devotos • 6 **masterful:** imperioso; autoritário • 7 **mischievous:** prejudicial; mal-intencionado • 8 **arch and saucy for the spinster:** malicioso e atrevido com a solteirona • 9 **gift:** dom • 10 **shamelessly:** sem vergonha; descaradamente • 11 **it was as much as he could do to prevent himself:** tinha de reprimir o instinto • 12 **taking a bow:** fazer uma reverência • 13 **thundering:** estrondoso • 14 **went rolling through:** atravessava • 15 **clownish quality:** seu lado bufão • 16 **it was said of him:** dizia-se dele • 17 **good taste:** bom gosto • 18 **reject:** rejeitar • 19 **ungraceful:** deselegante • 20 **drew the line:** estabelecia limites

from Chippendale's Chinese or Gothic period to come into his showroom, and the same was true of some of the heavier Italian designs of Robert Adam.

During the past few years, Mr. Boggis had achieved considerable fame among his friends in the trade by his ability to produce[1] unusual and often quite rare items[2] with astonishing regularity. Apparently the man had a source of supply that was almost inexhaustible[3], a sort of private warehouse[4], and it seemed that all he had to do was to drive out to it once a week and help himself[5]. Whenever they asked him where he got the stuff[6], he would smile knowingly[7] and wink[8] and murmur something about a little secret.

The idea behind Mr. Boggis's little secret was a simple one, and it had come to him as a result of something that had happened on a certain Sunday afternoon nearly nine years before, while he was driving in the country.

He had gone out in the morning to visit his old mother, who lived in Sevenoaks[9], and on the way back the fanbelt[10] on his car had broken, causing the engine to overheat and the water to boil away[11]. He had got out of the car and walked to the nearest house, a smallish[12] farm building about fifty yards[13] off the road[14] and had asked the woman who answered the door if he could please have a jug[15] of water.

1 **to produce:** apresentar; exibir • 2 **rare items:** itens raros • 3 **inexhaustible:** inesgotável • 4 **warehouse:** armazém; depósito • 5 **help himself:** servir-se • 6 **the stuff:** material • 7 **knowingly:** com astúcia • 8 **wink:** piscar os olhos • 9 **Sevenoaks:** pequena cidade situada a uns 35 km sudeste de Londres • 10 **fanbelt:** correia de motor • 11 **to boil away:** ferver até evaporar • 12 **smallish:** um tanto quanto pequena (o sufixo -ish é usado após um adjetivo com o sentido de "um tanto quanto"...) • 13 **fifty yards:** 45,73 metros (1 jarda = 0,91 m) • 14 **off the road:** fora da estrada • 15 **jug:** jarro; cântaro

While he was waiting for her to fetch it[1], he happened to glance in through the door to the living-room, and there, not five yards from where he was standing, he spotted something that made him so excited the sweat[2] began to come out all over the top of his head. It was a large oak armchair[3] of a type that he had only seen once before in his life. Each arm, as well as the panel at the back, was supported by a row of eight beautifully turned spindles[4]. The back panel itself was decorated by an inlay[5] of the most delicate floral design, and the head of a duck was carved[6] to lie along half the length of either arm. Good God[7] he thought. This thing is late fifteenth century[8]!

He poked his head in further[9] through the door, and there, by heavens[10], was another of them on the other side of the fireplace[11]!

He couldn't be sure, but two chairs like that must be worth at least a thousand pounds up in London. And oh, what beauties they were!

When the woman returned, Mr. Boggis introduced himself and straight away asked if she would like to sell her chairs.

Dear me[12], she said. But why on earth should she want to sell her chairs?

No reason at all, except that he might be willing to give her a pretty nice price.

---

1 **to fetch it:** para buscá-la • 2 **sweat:** suor • 3 **oak armchair:** poltrona de carvalho • 4 **beautifully turned spindles:** barras lindamente torneadas • 5 **inlay:** incrustação • 6 **carved:** talhada • 7 **good God:** Ó bom deus! • 8 **late fifteenth century:** finais do século XV • 9 **he poked his head in further:** colocou a cabeça para a frente • 10 **by heavens:** Ó céus! • 11 **fireplace:** lareira • 12 **dear me:** caramba

And how much would he give? They were definitely not for sale, but just out of curiosity, just for fun¹, you know, how much would he give?

Thirty-five pounds.

How much?

Thirty-five pounds.

Dear me, thirty-five pounds. Well, well, that was very interesting. She'd always thought they were valuable. They were very old. They were very comfortable too. She couldn't possibly do without them, not possibly. No, they were not for sale³ but thank you very much all the same³.

They weren't really so very old, Mr. Boggis told her, and they wouldn't be at all easy to sell, but it just happened⁴ that he had a client who rather liked that sort of thing. Maybe he could go up another two pounds—call it thirty-seven⁵. How about that?

They bargained⁶ for half an hour, and of course in the end Mr. Boggis got the chairs and agreed to pay her something less than a twentieth⁷ of their value.

That evening, driving back to London in his old station-wagon⁸ with the two fabulous chairs tucked away snugly⁹ in the back Mr. Boggis had suddenly been struck by what seemed to him to be a most remarkable idea¹⁰.

Look here, he said. If there is good stuff in one farmhouse,

---

1 **just for fun:** só por brincadeira • 2 **for sale:** à venda • 3 **all the same:** de todo modo; mesmo assim • 4 **it just so happened:** coincidentemente • 5 **call it thirty- seven:** digamos 37 • 6 **they bargained:** pechincharam • 7 **a twentieth:** uma vigésima parte • 8 **station-wagon:** perua • 9 **tucked away snugly:** confortavelmente encaixadas • 10 **had suddenly been struck by ... a most remarkable idea:** foi de repente tomado pelo que parecia ser a ideia mais extraordinária

then why not in others? Why shouldn't he search for it? Why shouldn't he comb the countryside[1]? He could do it on Sundays. In that way, it wouldn't interfere with his work at all. He never knew what to do with his Sundays.

So Mr. Boggis bought maps, large scale maps of all the counties around London, and with a fine pen he divided each of them up into a series of squares. Each of these squares covered an actual area of five miles by five, which was about as much territory, he estimated as he could cope with[2] on a single Sunday, were he to comb it thoroughly[3]. He didn't want the towns and the villages. It was the comparatively isolated places, the large farmhouses and the rather dilapidated country mansions, that he was looking for; and in this way, if he did one square each Sunday, fifty-two squares a year, he would gradually cover every farm and every country house in the home counties[4].

But obviously there was a bit more to it than that. Country folk are a suspicious lot[5] So are the impoverished[6] rich. You can't go about[7] ringing their bells and expecting them to show you around their houses[8] just for the asking[9], because they won't do it. That way you would never get beyond the front door. How then was he to gain admittance[10]? Perhaps it would be best if he didn't let them know he was a dealer

---

1 **comb the countryside:** rastrear a região rural • 2 **cope with:** poderia lidar • 3 **were he to comb it thoroughly:** se ele fosse rastrear por inteiro • 4 **the home counties:** os condados do sudeste da Inglaterra, próximos a Londres • 5 **country folk are a suspicious lot:** o pessoal do campo é bastante desconfiado • 6 **impoverished:** empobrecidos • 7 **go about:** ir por aí • 8 **to show you around their houses:** que mostrem as suas casas • 9 **just for the asking:** gratuitamente • 10 **to gain admittance:** ser autorizado a entrar

at all. He could be the telephone man, the plumber¹, the gas inspector. He could even be a clergyman. . . .

From this point on, the whole scheme began to take on a more practical aspect. Mr. Boggis ordered a large quantity of superior cards on which the following legend was engraved:

## THE REVEREND
## CYRIL WINNINGTON BOGGIS

| President of the Society for the Preservation of Rare Furniture | In association with The Victoria and Albert Museum² |

From now on, every Sunday, he was going to be a nice old parson³ spending his holiday travelling around on a labour of love for the "Society", compiling an inventory of the treasures that lay hidden⁴ in the country homes of England. And who in the world was going to kick him out⁵ when they heard that one?

Nobody.

And then, once he was inside, if he happened to spot something he really wanted, well—he knew a hundred different ways of dealing with that.

Rather to Mr. Boggis's surprise, the scheme worked⁶. In fact, the friendliness⁷ with which he was received in one house after another through the countryside was, in the

---

1 **plumber:** encanador • 2 **The Victoria and Albert Museum:** museu dedicado às artes aplicadas • 3 **parson:** pároco • 4 **lay hidden:** permaneciam ocultos • 5 **to kick him out:** expulsá-lo a pontapés • 6 **the scheme worked:** o esquema funcionou • 7 **friendliness:** amabilidade

beginning, quite embarrassing¹, even to him. A slice of cold pie², a glass of port³, a cup of tea, a basket of plums⁴, even a full sit-down Sunday dinner with the family, such things were constantly being pressed upon him. Sooner or later, of course, there had been some bad moments and a number of unpleasant incidents, but then nine years is more than four hundred Sundays, and that adds up to⁵ a great quantity of houses visited. All in all⁶, it had been an interesting, exciting, and lucrative business.

And now it was another Sunday and Mr. Boggis was operating in the county of Buckinghamshire, in one of the most northerly squares on his map, about ten miles from Oxford, and as he drove down the hill and headed for his first house, the dilapidated Queen Anne, he began to get the feeling that this was going to be one of his lucky days.

He parked the car about a hundred yards from the gates and got out to walk the rest of the way. He never liked people to see his car until after a deal was completed. A dear old clergyman and a large station-wagon somehow never seemed quite right together. Also the short walk gave him time to examine the property closely from the outside and to assume the mood most likely to be suitable for the occasion.

Mr. Boggis strode briskly up the drive⁷. He was a small fat-legged⁸ man with a belly⁹. The face was round and rosy¹⁰, quite perfect for the part¹¹, and the two large brown eyes that

---

1 **embarrassing:** embaraçosa • 2 **a slice of cold pie:** uma fatia de torta fria • 3 **port:** vinho do Porto • 4 **plums:** ameixas • 5 **that adds up to:** que somados resultam em • 6 **all in all:** no geral • 7 **strode briskly up the drive:** atravessou o caminho de entrada a passos largos • 8 **fat-legged:** com pernas grossas • 9 **belly:** barriga • 10 **rosy:** corada • 11 **for the part:** para o papel

bulged out at you[1] from this rosy face gave an impression of gentle imbecility. He was dressed in a black suit with the usual parson's dog-collar[2] round his neck and on his head a soft black hat. He carried an old oak walking-stick[3] which lent him[4], in his opinion, a rather rustic easy-going air[5].

He approached the front door and rang the bell. He heard the sound of footsteps in the hall and the door opened and suddenly there stood before him or rather above him, a gigantic woman dressed in riding-breeches[6]. Even through the smoke of her cigarette he could smell the powerful odour of stables and horse manure[7] that clung about[8] her.

"Yes?" she asked looking at him suspiciously. "What is it you want?"

Mr. Boggis, who half expected her to whinny[9] any moment, raised his hat, made a little bow, and handed her his card. "I do apologise for bothering you," he said and then he waited, watching her face as she read the message.

"I don't understand" she said, handing back the card. "What is it you want?"

Mr. Boggis explained about the Society for the Preservation of Rare Furniture.

"This wouldn't by any chance be something to do with the Socialist Party?" she asked, staring at him fiercely from under a pair of pale bushy brows[10].

---

1 **eyes that bulged out at you:** olhos enormes que saltavam sobre você • 2 **dog-collar:** colarinho de padre • 3 **walking-stick:** bengala • 4 **lent him:** lhe emprestava • 5 **easy-going air:** um ar despreocupado; à vontade • 6 **riding-breeches:** calças de montaria • 7 **manure:** esterco • 8 **clung about:** que se desprendia • 9 **whinny:** relinchar • 10 **bushy brows:** sobrancelhas espessas

From then on, it was easy. A Tory[1] in riding-breeches, male or female, was always a sitting duck[2] for Mr. Boggis. He spent two minutes delivering an impassioned eulogy on the extreme Right Wing of the Conservative Party, then two more denouncing the Socialists. As a clincher[3], he made particular reference to the Bill[4] that the Socialists had once introduced for the abolition of blood-sports[5] in the country, and went on to inform his listener that his idea of heaven —"though you better not tell the bishop, my dear"—was a place where one could hunt the fox, the stag, and the hare[6] with large packs of tireless hounds[7] from morn[8] till night every day of the week, including Sundays.

Watching her as he spoke, he could see the magic beginning to do its work. The woman was grinning[9] now, showing Mr. Boggis a set of enormous, slightly yellow teeth. "Madam," he cried "I beg of you[10] *please* don't get me started on Socialism." At that point, she let out a great guffaw of laughter[11], raised an enormous red hand, and slapped him so hard on the shoulder that he nearly went over.

"Come in!" she shouted "I don't know what the hell[12] you want but come on in!"

Unfortunately, and rather surprisingly, there was nothing of any value in the whole house, and Mr. Boggis, who never

---

1 **Tory:** do partido conservador inglês • 2 **a sitting duck:** uma presa fácil • 3 **clincher:** argumento decisivo • 4 **Bill:** projeto de lei • 5 **blood-sports:** esportes violentos • 6 **hunt the fox, the stag, and the hare:** caçar a raposa, o cervo e a lebre • 7 **packs of tireless hounds:** matilhas de cães incansáveis • 8 **morn (morning):** manhã • 9 **grinning:** sorrindo abertamente • 10 **I beg of you:** eu lhe suplico • 11 **guffaw of laughter:** gargalhada • 12 **what the hell:** que diabos

wasted time on barren[1] territory, soon made his excuses and took his leave. The whole visit had taken less than fifteen minutes, and that, he told himself as he climbed back into his car and started off for the next place, was exactly as it should be.

From now on it was all farmhouses, and the nearest was about half a mile up the road. It was a large half-timbered brick building[2] of considerable age, and there was a magnificent pear tree[3] still in blossom[4] covering almost the whole of the south wall.

Mr. Boggis knocked on the door. He waited, but no one came. He knocked again, but still there was no answer, so he wandered[5] around the back to look for the farmer among the cowsheds[6]. There was no one there either. He guessed that they must all still be in church, so he began peering[7] in the windows to see if he could spot anything interesting. There was nothing in the dining-room. Nothing in the library either. He tried the next window, the living-room, and there, right under his nose[8], in the little alcove[9] that the window made, he saw a beautiful thing, a semi-circular card-table in mahogany[10], richly veneered[11], and in the style of Hepplewhite, built around 1780.

"Ah-ha," he said aloud, pressing his face hard against glass. "Well done, Boggis."

---

1 **barren:** estéril; infrutífero • 2 **half-timbered brick building:** construção de madeira e tijolos • 3 **pear tree:** pereira • 4 **in blossom:** em flor • 5 **wandered:** passeou • 6 **cowsheds:** estábulos de vacas • 7 **peering:** observar atentamente • 8 **right under his nose:** bem debaixo do seu nariz • 9 **alcove:** nicho • 10 **mahogany:** mogno • 11 **veneered:** marchetada

But that was not all. There was a chair there as well, a single chair, and if he were not mistaken it was of an even finer quality than the table. Another Hepplewhite, wasn't it? And oh, what a beauty! The lattices[1] on the back were finely carved with the honeysuckle[2], the husk[3], and the paterae[4], the caning[5] on the seat was original, the legs were very gracefully turned and the two back ones had that peculiar outward splay[6] that meant so much. It was an exquisite chair. "Before this day is done," Mr. Boggis said softly, "I shall have the pleasure of sitting down upon that lovely seat." He never bought a chair without doing this. It was a favourite test of his, and it was always an intriguing sight to see him lowering himself[7] delicately into the seat, waiting for the "give", expertly gauging[8] the precise but infinitesimal degree of shrinkage[9] that the years had caused in the mortice and dovetail joints[10].

But there was no hurry, he told himself. He would return here later. He had the whole afternoon before him.

The next farm was situated some way back in the fields, and in order to keep his car out of sight Mr. Boggis had to leave it on the road and walk about six hundred yards along a straight track that led directly into the back yard of the farmhouse. This place, he noticed as he approached, was a good deal[11] smaller than the last, and he didn't hold out much hope

---

1 **lattices:** treliças • 2 **honeysuckle:** madressilva • 3 **husk:** casca (de milho); fibra vegetal • 4 **paterae:** patera (ornamento circular semelhante a um prato) • 5 **caning:** vime entrelaçado • 6 **outward splay:** acabamento externo chanfrado • 7 **lowering himself:** agachando-se • 8 **gauging:** aferindo • 9 **shrinkage:** encolhimento; contração • 10 **the mortice and dovetail joints:** malhete (encaixe em forma de rabo de andorinha) • 11 **a good deal:** bastante

for it¹. It looked rambling² and dirty, and some of the sheds³ were clearly in bad repair⁴.

There were three men standing in a close group in a corner of the yard⁵, and one of them had two large black greyhounds with him on leashes⁶. When the men caught sight of⁷ Mr. Boggis walking forward in his black suit and parson's collar, they stopped talking and seemed suddenly to stiffen⁸ and freeze⁹, becoming absolutely still, motionless, three faces turned towards him, watching him suspiciously as he approached.

The oldest of the three was a stumpy¹⁰ man with a wide frog mouth¹¹ and small shifty eyes¹², and although Mr. Boggis didn't know it his name was Rummins and he was the owner of the farm.

The tall youth¹³ beside him, who appeared to have something wrong with one eye, was Bert, the son of Rummins.

The shortish fat-faced man with a narrow corrugated brow¹⁴ and immensely broad shoulders was Claud. Claud had dropped in on¹⁵ Rummins in the hope of getting a piece of pork¹⁶ or ham out of him from the pig that had been killed the day before. Claud knew about the killing¹⁷—the noise of it had carried far across the fields—and he also knew that

---

1 **he didn't hold out much hope for it:** não apostava muito naquele lugar • 2 **rambling:** tortuoso • 3 **sheds:** coberturas; telhados • 4 **in bad repair:** em más condições • 5 **yard:** pátio • 6 **greyhounds on leashes:** cães galgos presos com coleiras • 7 **caught sight of:** notaram a presença • 8 **stiffen:** tensos • 9 **freeze:** paralisados • 10 **stumpy:** atarracado • 11 **a wide frog mouth:** uma enorme boca de sapo • 12 **shifty eyes:** olhos espertos • 13 **youth:** jovem • 14 **corrugated brow:** de testa e sobrancelhas franzidas • 15 **had dropped in on:** apareceu no local • 16 **pork:** carne de porco • 17 **killing:** matança; abate

a man should have a government permit to do that sort of thing, and that Rummins didn't have one.

"Good afternoon," Mr. Boggis said. "Isn't it a lovely day?" None of the three men moved. At that moment they were all thinking precisely the same thing—that somehow or other this clergyman who was certainly not the local fellow[1], had been sent to poke his nose into their business[2] and to report what he found to the government.

"What beautiful dogs," Mr. Boggis said. "I must say I've never been greyhound-racing myself, but they tell me it's a fascinating sport."

Again the silence, and Mr. Boggis glanced quickly from Rummins to Bert, then to Claud, then back again to Rummins, and he noticed that each of them had the same peculiar expression on his face, something between a jeer[3] and a challenge[4], with a contemptuous curl to the mouth[5] and a sneer[6] around the nose.

"Might I inquire if you are the owner?" Mr. Boggis asked, undaunted[7], addressing himself to Rummins.

"What is it you want?"

"I do apologize for troubling you, especially on a Sunday."

Mr. Boggis offered his card and Rummins took it and held it up close to his face. The other two didn't move, but their eyes swivelled over to one side[8], trying to see.

---

1 **the local fellow:** o clérigo local • 2 **poke his nose into their business:** enfiar seu nariz nos assuntos deles • 3 **jeer:** gozação; escárnio; zombaria • 4 **challenge:** desafio • 5 **with a contemptuous curl to the mouth:** com uma expressão de desprezo • 6 **a sneer:** um olhar sarcástico; de desdém • 7 **undaunted:** destemido • 8 **their eyes swivelled over to one side:** seus olhos se voltaram para um lado

"And what exactly might you be wanting?" Rummins asked.

For the second time that morning, Mr. Boggis explained at some length[1] the aims and ideals of the Society for the Preservation of Rare Furniture.

"We don't have any," Rummins told him when it was over. "You're wasting your time."

"Now, just a minute, sir," Mr. Boggis said raising a finger. "The last man who said that to me was an old farmer down in Sussex, and when he finally let me into his house, d'you know what I found? A dirty-looking old chair in the corner of the kitchen, and it turned out to be worth[2] *four hundred pounds*! I showed him how to sell it, and he bought himself a new tractor with the money."

"What on earth are you talking about?" Claud said. "There ain't no chair[3] in the world worth four hundred pound."

"Excuse me," Mr. Boggis answered primly[4], "but there are plenty of chairs in England worth more than twice that figure[5]. And you know where they are? They're tucked away[6] in the farms and cottages all over the country, with the owners using them as steps and ladders and standing on them with hobnailed boots[7] to reach a pot of jam[8] out of the top cupboard or to hang a picture. This is the truth I'm telling you, my friends."

---

1 **at some length:** com bastante detalhe ou demoradamente • 2 **it turned out to be worth:** se verificou que valia • 3 **there ain't no (there isn't any) chair:** não existe nenhuma cadeira • 4 **primly:** afetadamente • 5 **twice that figure**: o dobro deste montante • 6 **tucked away:** guardadinhas • 7 **hobnailed boots:** botas com pregos na sola • 8 **a pot of jam:** um pote de geleia

Rummins shifted uneasily on his feet[1]. "You mean to say all you want to do is go inside and stand there in the middle of the room and look around?"

"Exactly," Mr. Boggis said. He was at last beginning to sense what the trouble might be. "I don't want to pry[2] into your cupboards or into your larder[3]. I just want to look at the furniture to see if you happen to have any treasures here, and then I can write about them in our Society magazine."

"You know what I think?" Rummins said, fixing him with his small wicked[4] eyes. "I think you're after buying[5] the stuff yourself. Why else would you be going to all this trouble?"

"Oh, dear me. I only wish I had the money. Of course, if I saw something that I took a great fancy to[6], and it wasn't beyond my means[7], I might be tempted to make an offer. But alas[8], that rarely happens."

"Well," Rummins said "I don't suppose there's any harm in your taking a look around if that's all you want." He led the way across the yard to the back door of the farmhouse, and Mr. Boggis followed him; so did the son Bert, and Claud with his two dogs. They went through the kitchen, where the only furniture was a cheap deal[9] table with a dead chicken lying on it, and they emerged into a fairly large, exceedingly filthy[10] living-room.

---

1 **shifted uneasily on his feet:** se mexeu impacientemente sobre seus pés • 2 **to pry:** intrometer-se; fuçar • 3 **larder:** despensa • 4 **wicked:** malvados • 5 **you're after buying:** você pretende comprar • 6 **I took a great fancy to:** que caiu no meu agrado • 7 **beyond my means:** além das minhas possibilidades • 8 **but alas:** mas infelizmente • 9 **deal:** pinho • 10 **exceedingly filthy:** incrivelmente imunda

And there it was! Mr. Boggis saw it at once, and he stopped dead in his tracks[1] and gave a little shrill gasp of shock[2]. Then he stood there for five, ten, fifteen seconds at least, staring like an idiot, unable to believe, not daring to[3] believe what he saw before him. It *couldn't* be true, not possibly! But the longer he stared, the more true it began to seem. After all, there it was standing against the wall right in front of him, as real and as solid as the house itself. And who in the world could possibly make a mistake about a thing like that? Admittedly[4] it was painted white, but that made not the slightest difference. Some idiot had done that. The paint could easily be stripped off[5]. But good God! Just look at it! And in a place like this!

At this point Mr. Boggis became aware of the three men, Rummins, Bert, and Claud, standing together in a group over by the fireplace, watching him intently[6]. They had seen him stop and gasp and stare, and they must have seen his face turning red or maybe it was white, but in any event they had seen enough to spoil[7] the whole goddamn business if he didn't do something about it quick. In a flash[8], Mr. Boggis clapped[9] one hand over his heart, staggered[10] to the nearest chair, and collapsed into it breathing heavily.

"What's the matter with you?" Claud asked.

"It's nothing," he gasped. "I'll be all right in a minute.

---

1 **he stopped dead in his tracks:** ele ficou pasmo • 2 **a little shrill gasp of shock:** um pequeno grito agudo e ofegante de surpresa • 3 **not daring to:** não se atrevendo a • 4 **admittedly:** tinha de reconhecer que • 5 **stripped off:** arrancada; descascada • 6 **intently:** atentamente • 7 **spoil:** estragar • 8 **in a flash:** em um lampejo • 9 **clapped:** bateu a mão • 10 **staggered:** cambaleou; titubeou

Please—a glass of water. It's my heart."

Bert fetched[1] him the water, handed it to him, and stayed close beside him, staring down at him with a fatuous leer[2] on his face.

"I thought maybe you were looking at something," Rummins said. The wide frog-mouth widened a fraction further into a crafty grin[3], showing the stubs[4] of several broken teeth.

"No, no," Mr. Boggis said. "Oh dear me, no. It's just my heart. I'm so sorry. It happens every now and then. But it goes away quite quickly. I'll be all right in a couple of minutes."

He *must* have time to think, he told himself. More important still, he must have time to compose himself thoroughly before he said another word. Take it gently, Boggis. And whatever you do, keep calm. These people may be ignorant, but they are not stupid. They are suspicious and wary[5] and sly[6]. And if it is really true—no it *can't* be, it *can't* be true . . .

He was holding one hand up over his eyes in a gesture of pain, and now, very carefully, secretly, he made a little crack[7] between two of the fingers and peeked[8] through.

Sure enough, the thing was still there, and on this occasion he took a good long look at it. Yes—he had been right the first time! There wasn't the slightest doubt about it! It was really unbelievable!

What he saw was a piece of furniture that any expert would have given almost anything to acquire. To a layman[9],

---

1 **fetched:** foi buscar • 2 **a fatuous leer:** um olhar tolo • 3 **a crafty grin:** um sorriso astuto • 4 **stubs:** tocos • 5 **wary:** cautelosos • 6 **sly:** astutos • 7 **crack:** estalo • 8 **peeked:** espiou ao redor • 9 **to a layman:** para um leigo

it might not have appeared particularly impressive, especially when covered over as it was with dirty white paint but to Mr. Boggis it was a dealer's dream. He knew, as does every other dealer in Europe and America, that among the most celebrated and coveted[1] examples of eighteenth-century English furniture in existence are the three famous pieces known as "The Chippendale Commodes[2]". He knew their history backwards[3]—that the first was "discovered" in 1920, in a house at Moreton-in-Marsh, and was sold at Sotheby's the same year; that the other two turned up[4] in the same auction rooms[5] a year later, both coming out of Raynham Hall, Norfolk. They all fetched[6] enormous prices. He couldn't quite remember the exact figure for the first one, or even the second, but he knew for certain that the last one to be sold had fetched thirty-nine hundred guineas[7]. And that was in 1921! Today the same piece would surely be worth ten thousand pounds. Some man, Mr. Boggis couldn't remember his name, had made a study of these commodes fairly[8] recently and had proved that all three must have come from the same workshop[9], for the veneers[10] were all from the same log[11], and the same set of templates[12] had been used in the construction of each. No invoices[13] had been found for any of them but all the experts were agreed that these three commodes could have been executed only by Thomas Chippen-

---

1 **coveted:** cobiçados • 2 **commodes:** cômodas • 3 **he knew their history backwards:** ele conhecia sua história de trás para a frente • 4 **turned up:** apareceram • 5 **auction rooms:** salas de leilão • 6 **fetched:** alcançaram • 7 **guinea:** antiga moeda inglesa • 8 **fairly:** bastante • 9 **workshop:** oficina (de marcenaria) • 10 **veneers:** marchetarias • 11 **log:** tronco • 12 **template:** molde • 13 **invoices:** faturas

dale himself, with his own hands, at the most exalted period in his career.

And here, Mr. Boggis kept telling himself as he peered cautiously through the crack in his fingers, here was the fourth Chippendale Commode! And *he* had found it! He would be rich! He would also be famous! Each of the other three was known throughout the furniture world by a special name—The Chastleton Commode, The First Raynham Commode, The Second Raynham Commode. This one would go down in history[1] as The Boggis Commode! Just imagine the faces of the boys up there in London when they got a look at it tomorrow morning! And the luscious[2] offers coming in from the big fellows over in the West End—Frank Partridge, Mallett, Jetley, and the rest of them! There would be a picture of it in *The Times*[3], and it would say, "The very fine Chippendale Commode which was recently discovered by Mr. Cyril Boggis, a London dealer. . . ." Dear God, what a stir[4] he was going to make!

This one here, Mr. Boggis thought, was almost exactly similar to the Second Raynham Commode. (All three, the Chastleton and the two Raynhams, differed[5] from one another in a number of small ways.) It was a most impressive, handsome affair[6], built in the French rococo style of Chippendale's Directoire period, a kind of large fat chest-of-drawers[7] set upon four carved and fluted[8] legs that raised it about a foot from the ground. There were six drawers[9] in all,

---

1 **go down in history:** passaria para a História • 2 **luscious:** sedutoras • 3 ***The Times*:** jornal inglês • 4 **what a stir:** que rebuliço • 5 **differed:** se diferenciavam • 6 **handsome affair:** um belo objeto • 7 **chest-of-drawers:** cômoda • 8 **fluted:** caneladas • 9 **drawers:** gavetas

two long ones in the middle and two shorter ones on either side. The serpentine front was magnificently ornamented along the top and sides and bottom, and also vertically between each set of drawers, with intricate carvings of festoons[1] and scrolls[2] and clusters[3]. The brass handles[4], although partly obscured by white paint, appeared to be superb[5]. It was, of course, a rather "heavy" piece, but the design had been executed with such elegance and grace that the heaviness was in no way offensive.

"How're you feeling now?" Mr. Boggis heard someone saying.

"Thank you, thank you, I'm much better already. It passes quickly. My doctor says it's nothing to worry about really so long as I rest for a few minutes whenever it happens. Ah yes," he said, raising himself slowly to his feet. "That's better. I'm all right now."

A trifle unsteadily[6], he began to move around the room examining the furniture, one piece at a time, commenting upon it briefly. He could see at once that apart from the commode it was a very poor lot.

"Nice oak table," he said. "But I'm afraid it's not old enough to be of any interest. Good comfortable chairs, but quite modern, yes, quite modern. Now this cupboard, well, it's rather attractive, but again, not valuable. This chest-of-drawers"—he walked casually[7] past the Chippendale Commode and gave it a little contemptuous flip[8] with

---

1 **festoons:** festões; grinaldas • 2 **scrolls:** volutas; arabescos • 3 **clusters:** cachos • 4 **the brass handles:** puxadores de bronze • 5 **superb:** soberbos; magníficos • 6 **a trifle unsteadily:** ligeiramente inseguro; vacilante • 7 **casually:** casualmente • 8 **flip:** pancadinha

his fingers—"worth a few pounds, I dare say, but no more. A rather crude[1] reproduction, I'm afraid. Probably made in Victorian times. Did you paint it white?"

"Yes," Rummins said, "Bert did it."

"A very wise move. It's considerably less offensive in white."

"That's a strong piece of furniture," Rummins said. "Some nice carving[2] on it too."

"Machine-carved" Mr. Boggis answered superbly[3], bending down to examine the exquisite craftsmanship[4]. "You can tell it a mile off[5]. But still, I suppose it's quite pretty in its way. It has its points."

He began to saunter off[6], then he checked himself[7] and turned slowly back again. He placed the tip[8] of one finger against the point of his chin, laid his head over to one side, and frowned as though deep in thought.

"You know what?" he said, looking at the commode, speaking so casually that his voice kept trailing off[9]. "I've just remembered ... I've been wanting a set[10] of legs something like that for a long time. I've got a rather curious table in my own little home, one of those low things that people put in front of the sofa, sort of a coffee-table, and last Michaelmas[11], when I moved house, the foolish movers[12] damaged the legs in the most shocking[13] way. I'm very fond of[14] that table.

---

1 **crude:** grosseira • 2 **carving:** entalhes • 3 **superbly:** com soberba • 4 **craftsmanship:** obra de arte • 5 **you can tell it a mile off:** pode-se perceber a léguas • 6 **saunter off:** a se afastar tranquilamente • 7 **he checked himself:** parou de repente • 8 **tip:** ponta • 9 **kept trailing off:** foi se apagando • 10 **a set:** um jogo • 11 **Michaelmas:** Missa do dia de São Miguel • 12 **movers:** rapazes da mudança • 13 **shocking:** horrível • 14 **I'm very fond of:** tenho especial carinho

I always keep my big Bible on it, and all my sermon notes."

He paused, stroking¹ his chin with the finger. "Now I was just thinking. These legs on your chest-of-drawers might be very suitable². Yes, they might indeed. They could easily be cut off and fixed on to my table."

He looked around and saw the three men standing absolutely still³, watching him suspiciously, three pairs of eyes, all different but equally mistrusting⁴, small pig-eyes for Rummins, large slow eyes for Claud, and two odd⁵ eyes for Bert, one of them very queer⁶ and boiled⁷ and misty pale⁸, with a little black dot in the centre, like a fish eye on a plate.

Mr. Boggis smiled and shook his head. "Come, come⁹, what on earth am I saying? I'm talking as though I owned the piece myself. I do apologize."

"What you mean to say is you'd like to buy it," Rummins said.

"Well ... " Mr. Boggis glanced back at the commode, frowning¹⁰. "I'm not sure. I might ... and then again ... on second thoughts¹¹ ... no ... I think it might be a bit too much trouble. It's not worth it. I'd better leave it."

"How much were you thinking of offering?" Rummins asked.

"Not much, I'm afraid. You see, this is not a genuine antique. It's merely a reproduction¹²."

---

1 **stroking:** acariciando • 2 **suitable:** apropriadas • 3 **still:** parados; quietos • 4 **mistrusting:** desconfiados • 5 **odd:** diferentes entre si • 6 **queer:** esquisito • 7 **boiled:** saliente • 8 **misty pale:** pálido e nebuloso • 9 **come, come:** veja, veja • 10 **frowning:** franzindo as sobrancelhas • 11 **on second thoughts:** pensando bem • 12 **merely a reproduction:** meramente uma reprodução

"I'm not so sure about that," Rummins told him. "It's been in *here* over twenty years, and before that it was up at the Manor House¹. I bought it there myself at auction when the old Squire² died. You can't tell me that thing's new."

"It's not exactly new, but it's certainly not more than about sixty years old."

"It's more than that," Rummins said. "Bert, where's that bit of paper you once found at the back of one of them drawers? That old bill."

The boy looked vacantly³ at his father.

Mr. Boggis opened his mouth, then quickly shut it again without uttering a sound⁴. He was beginning literally to shake with excitement, and to calm himself he walked over to the window and stared out at a plump brown hen⁵ pecking around for stray grains⁶ of corn in the yard.

"It was in the back of that drawer underneath all them rabbit-snares⁷," Rummins was saying. "Go on and fetch it out and show it to the parson."

When Bert went forward to the commode, Mr. Boggis turned round again. He couldn't stand not watching him. He saw him pull out one of the big middle drawers, and he noticed the beautiful way in which the drawer slid open⁸. He saw Bert's hand dipping inside and rummaging⁹ around among a lot of wires and strings.

---

1 **the Manor House:** solar; casa-grande • 2 **Squire:** nobre rural • 3 **vacantly:** com expressão ausente • 4 **without uttering a sound:** sem emitir um som • 5 **a plump brown hen:** uma galinha marrom e rechonchuda • 6 **pecking around for stray grains:** bicando grãos espalhados • 7 **rabbit-snares:** armadilhas de coelho • 8 **slid open:** deslizou e abriu • 9 **rummaging:** remexendo

"You mean this?" Bert lifted out a piece of folded yellowing paper[1] and carried it over to the father, who unfolded it and held it up close to his face.

"You can't tell me this writing ain't bloody old[2]," Rummins said, and he held the paper out to Mr. Boggis, whose whole arm was shaking as he took it. It was brittle[3] and it crackled[4] slightly between his fingers. The writing was in a long sloping copperplate hand[5]:

Edward Montagu, Esq.[6]                  Dr
                                         To Thos.[7] Chippendale

A large mahogany Commode Table of exceeding fine wood very rich carvd[8] set upon fluted legs, two very neat shaped[9] long drawers in the middle part and two ditto[10] on each side, with rich chasd[11] Brass Handles and Ornaments, the whole completely finished in the most exquisite taste .......... £ 87

Mr. Boggis was holding on to himself tight and fighting to suppress the excitement that was spinning round[12] inside him and making him dizzy[13]. Oh God, it was wonderful! With the invoice[14], the value had climbed even higher. What in heaven's name[15] would it fetch now? Twelve thousand

---

1 **folded yellowing paper:** um papel amarelado dobrado • 2 **bloody old:** muito antigo (forma vulgar de falar) • 3 **brittle:** frágil; quebradiço • 4 **it crackled:** crepitou levemente • 5 **sloping copperplate hand:** caligrafia inclinada • 6 **Esq. (Esquire):** forma educada de se dirigir a um homem (senhor) • 7 **Thos:** Thomas • 8 **carvd (carved):** entalhado • 9 **shaped:** em forma de • 10 **ditto:** iguais; idem • 11 **chasd:** lavrado • 12 **spinning round:** girava • 13 **dizzy:** atordoado • 14 **invoice:** fatura • 15 **in heaven's name:** pelo amor de Deus

pounds? Fourteen? Maybe fifteen or even twenty? Who knows?

Oh, boy!

He tossed[1] the paper contemptuously[2] on to the table and said quietly, "It's exactly what I told you, a Victorian reproduction. This is simply the invoice that the seller—the man who made it and passed it off as an antique[3]—gave to his client. I've seen lots of them. You'll notice that he doesn't say he made it himself. That would give the game away[4]."

"Say what you like," Rummins announced, "but that's an old piece of paper."

"Of course it is, my dear friend. It's Victorian[5], late Victorian. About eighteen ninety. Sixty or seventy years old. I've seen hundreds of them. That was a time when masses of cabinetmakers[6] did nothing else but apply themselves to faking[7] the fine furniture of the century before."

"Listen, Parson," Rummins said, pointing at him with a thick dirty finger, "I'm not saying as how you may not know a fair bit[8] about this furniture business, but what I am saying is this: How on earth can you be so mighty sure[9] it's a fake when you haven't even seen what it looks like underneath all that paint?"

"Come here," Mr. Boggis said. "Come over here and I'll show you." He stood beside the commode and waited for them to gather round[10]. "Now, anyone got a knife?"

---

1 **he tossed:** ele jogou • 2 **contemptuously:** com desdém • 3 **passed it off as antique:** a fez passar como se fosse uma antiguidade • 4 **give the game away:** entregar a farsa, a fraude • 5 **Victorian:** hoje, praticamente sinônimo do século XIX • 6 **masses of cabinetmakers:** um monte de marceneiros • 7 **faking:** falsificar • 8 **a fair bit:** um bocado de coisas • 9 **so mighty sure:** tão convencido • 10 **gather round:** se juntarem ao redor

Claud produced[1] a horn-handled[2] pocket knife, and Mr. Boggis took it and opened the smallest blade[3]. Then, working with apparent casualness but actually with extreme care, he began chipping off[4] the white paint from a small area on the top of the commode. The paint flaked away[5] cleanly from the old hard varnish underneath, and when he had cleared away about three square inches, he stepped back and said, "Now, take a look at that!"

It was beautiful—a warm little patch[6] of mahogany, glowing like a topaz, rich and dark with the true colour of its two hundred years.

"What's wrong with it?" Rummins asked

"It's processed! anyone can see that!"

"How can you see it, Mister? You tell us."

"Well, I must say that's a trifle difficult to explain. It's chiefly[7] a matter of experience. My experience tells me that without the slightest doubt this wood has been processed with lime[8]. That's what they use for mahogany, to give it that dark aged colour. For oak, they use potash salts[9], and for walnut[10] it's nitric acid but for mahogany it's always lime."

The three men moved a little closer to peer at the wood. There was a slight stirring[11] of interest among them now. It was always intriguing to hear about some new form of crookery[12] or deception[13].

---

1 **produced:** sacou; tirou • 2 **horn-handled:** cabo de chifre • 3 **blade:** lâmina • 4 **he began chipping off:** começou a tirar lascas • 5 **flaked away:** sair em lascas • 6 **patch:** pedaço • 7 **chiefly:** principalmente • 8 **lime:** cal • 9 **potash salts:** sais de potássio • 10 **walnut:** nogueira • 11 **stirring:** indício (movimento) • 12 **crookery:** trapaça • 13 **deception:** engano

"Look closely at the grain¹. You see that touch of orange in among the dark red-brown. That's the sign of lime."

They leaned forward, their noses close to the wood, first Rummins, then Claud, then Bert.

"And then there's the patina," Mr. Boggis continued.

"The what?"

He explained to them the meaning of this words applied to furniture.

"My dear friends, you've no idea the trouble these rascals² will go to to imitate the hard beautiful bronze-like appearance of genuine patina. It's terrible, really terrible, and it makes me quite sick to speak of it!" He was spitting³ each word sharply off the tip of the tongue and making a sour mouth⁴ to show his extreme distaste. The men waited, hoping for more secrets.

"The time and trouble that some mortals will go to in order to deceive the innocent!" Mr. Boggis cried. "It's perfectly disgusting! D'you know what they did here, my friends? I can recognise it clearly. I can almost *see* them doing it, the long, complicated ritual of rubbing the wood with linseed oil⁵, coating it⁶ over with french polish⁷ that has been cunningly⁸ coloured, brushing it down with pumice-stone⁹ and oil, bees-waxing it¹⁰ with a wax that contains dirt and dust and finally giving it the heat treatment to crack the polish

---

1 **grain:** veio da madeira • 2 **rascals:** tratantes • 3 **spitting:** cuspindo • 4 **making a sour mouth:** com expressão azeda na boca • 5 **linseed oil:** óleo de linhaça • 6 **coating it:** revestindo • 7 **french polish:** polimento francês (técnica de acabamento para madeiras) • 8 **cunningly:** astutamente • 9 **brushing it down with pumice-stone:** polindo com pedra-pomes • 10 **bees-waxing it:** encerando com cera de abelha

so that it looks like two-hundred-year-old varnish! It really upsets me to contemplate such knavery[1]!"

The three men continued to gaze at[2] the little patch of dark wood.

"Feel it!" Mr. Boggis ordered. "Put your fingers on it! There, how does it feel, warm or cold?"

"Feels cold," Rummins said.

"Exactly, my friend! It happens to be a fact that faked patina is always cold to the touch. Real patina has a curiously warm feel to it."

"This feels normal," Rummins said, ready to argue.

"No, sir, it's cold. But of course it takes[3] an experienced and sensitive finger-tip[4] to pass a positive judgement[5]. You couldn't really be expected to judge this any more than I could[6] be expected to judge the quality of your barley[7]. Everything in life, my dear sir, is experience."

The men were staring at this queer moon-faced[8] clergyman with the bulging eyes, not quite so suspiciously now because he did seem to know a bit about his subject. But they were still a long way from trusting him.

Mr. Boggis bent down and pointed to one of the metal drawer-handles on the commode. "This is another place where the fakers go to work," he said. "Old brass normally has a colour and character all of its own. Did you know that?"

---

1 **knavery:** desonestidade • 2 **to gaze at:** contemplar • 3 **it takes:** é preciso; é necessário • 4 **finger-tip:** ponta do dedo • 5 **to pass a positive judgement:** dar uma opinião fidedigna • 6 **any more than I could:** tanto quanto eu não poderia • 7 **barley:** cevada • 8 **moon-faced:** com cara de lua

They stared at him, hoping for still more secrets.

"But the trouble is that they've become exceedingly skilled at matching it[1]. In fact, it's almost impossible to tell the difference between 'genuine old' and 'faked old'. I don't mind admitting that it has me guessing[2]. So there's not really any point in our scraping[3] the paint off these handles. We wouldn't be any the wiser[4]."

"How can you possibly make new brass look like old?" Claud said. "Brass doesn't rust[5], you know."

"You are quite right, my friend. But these scoundrels[6] have their own secret methods."

"Such as what?" Claud asked. Any information of this nature was valuable, in his opinion. One never knew when it might come in handy[7].

"All they have to do," Mr. Boggis said "is to place these handles overnight[8] in a box of mahogany shavings[9] saturated in sal ammoniac. The sal ammoniac turns the metal green but if you rub off the green, you will find underneath it a fine soft silvery-warm lustre, a lustre identical to that which comes with very old brass. Oh, it is so bestial, the things they do! With iron they have another trick[10]."

"What do they do with iron?" Claud asked, fascinated.

"Iron's easy," Mr. Boggis said. "Iron locks[11] and plates[12]

---

1 **matching it:** imitá-lo • 2 **it has me guessing:** me deixa na dúvida • 3 **in our scraping the paint:** ao descascarmos a pintura • 4 **we wouldn't be any the wiser:** não ficaríamos mais esclarecidos • 5 **rust:** oxidar; enferrujar • 6 **scoundrels:** tratantes; malandros • 7 **come in handy:** ser útil • 8 **overnight:** durante toda a noite • 9 **shavings:** raspas; cavacos • 10 **trick:** truque • 11 **locks:** fechaduras • 12 **plates:** chapas; placas

and hinges[1] are simply buried in common salt and they come out all rusted and pitted[2] in no time[3]."

"All right," Rummins said. "So you admit you can't tell about the handles. For all you know, they may be hundreds and hundreds of years old. Correct?"

"Ah," Mr. Boggis whispered[4], fixing Rummins with two big bulging brown eyes. "That's where you're wrong. Watch this."

From his jacket pocket, he took out a small screwdriver[5]. At the same time, although none of them saw him do it, he also took out a little brass screw which he kept well hidden in the palm of his hand. Then he selected one of the screws[6] in the commode—there were four to each handle—and began carefully scraping all traces of white paint from its head. When he had done this, he started slowly to unscrew[7] it.

"If this is a genuine old brass screw from the eighteenth century," he was saying, "the spiral will be slightly uneven[8] and you'll be able to see quite easily that it has been hand-cut with a file[9]. But if this brasswork is faked from more recent times, Victorian or later, then obviously the screw will be of the same period. It will be a mass-produced, machine-made article. Anyone can recognise a machine-made screw. Well, we shall see."

It was not difficult, as he put his hands over the old screw and drew it out[10], for Mr. Boggis to substitute the new one

---

1 **hinges:** dobradiças • 2 **pitted:** marcados • 3 **in no time:** em pouco tempo • 4 **whispered:** murmurou • 5 **screwdriver:** chave de fenda • 6 **screws:** parafusos • 7 **to unscrew:** desparafusar • 8 **uneven:** torta • 9 **file:** lima • 10 **drew it out:** tirou-o

hidden in his palm. This was another little trick of his, and through the years it had proved a most rewarding[1] one. The pockets of his clergyman's jacket were always stocked with[2] a quantity of cheap brass screws of various sizes.

"There you are," he said handing the modern screw to Rummins. "Take a look at that. Notice the exact evenness[3] of the spiral? See it? Of course you do. It's just a cheap common little screw you yourself could buy today in any ironmonger's[4] in the country."

The screw was handed round from the one to the other, each examining it carefully. Even Rummins was impressed now. Mr. Boggis put the screwdriver back in his pocket together with the fine hand-cut screw that he'd taken from the commode, and then he turned and walked slowly past the three men towards the door.

"My dear friends," he said, pausing at the entrance to the kitchen, "it was so good of you to let me peep[5] inside your little home—so kind. I do hope I haven't been a terrible old bore[6]."

Rummins glanced up from examining the screw. "You didn't tell us what you were going to offer," he said.

"Ah," Mr. Boggis said. "That's quite right. I didn't, did I? Well, to tell you the honest truth, I think it's all a bit too much trouble. I think I'll leave it."

"How much would you give?"

"You mean that you really wish to part with[7] it?"

---

1 **rewarding:** recompensador; proveitoso • 2 **stocked with:** abastecidos de • 3 **evenness:** regularidade • 4 **ironmonger's:** casa de ferragens • 5 **peep:** espiar • 6 **bore:** chato • 7 **to part with:** se desfazer de

"I didn't say I wished to part with it. I asked you how much."

Mr. Boggis looked across at the commode, and he laid his head first to one side, then to the other, and he frowned, and pushed out his lips, and shrugged his shoulders[1], and gave a little scornful[2] wave of the hand[3] as though to say the thing was hardly worth thinking about[4] really, was it?

"Shall we say . . . ten pounds. I think that would be fair."

"Ten pounds!" Rummins cried, "Don't be so ridiculous, Parson, *please!*"

"It's worth more'n[5] that for firewood[6]!" Claud said, disgusted.

"Look here at the bill!" Rummins went on, stabbing[7] that precious document so fiercely with his dirty fore-finger[8] that Mr. Boggis became alarmed. "It tells you exactly what it cost! Eighty-seven pounds! And that's when it was new. Now it's antique it's worth double!"

"If you'll pardon me, no, sir, it's not. It's a second-hand reproduction. But I'll tell you what, my friend—I'm being rather reckless[9], I can't help it—I'll go up as high as fifteen pounds. How's that?"

"Make it fifty[10]," Rummins said.

A delicious little quiver[11] like needles[12] ran all the way down the back of Mr. Boggis's legs and then under the soles

---

1 **shrugged his shoulders:** deu de ombros • 2 **scornful:** desdenhoso • 3 **wave of the hand:** aceno com a mão • 4 **the thing was hardly worth thinking about:** quase não valia a pena pensar nisso • 5 **more'n (more than):** mais que • 6 **firewood:** lenha • 7 **stabbing:** cravando • 8 **fore-finger:** dedo indicador • 9 **reckless:** temerário • 10 **make if fifty:** que sejam cinquenta • 11 **quiver:** tremor • 12 **needles:** agulhas

of his feet[1]. He had it now. It was his. No question about that. But the habit of buying cheap, as cheap as it was humanly possible to buy, acquired by years of necessity and practice, was too strong in him now to permit him to give in[2] so easily.

"My dear man" he whispered softly, "I only *want* the legs. Possibly I could find some use for the drawers later on, but the rest of it the carcass itself, as your friend so rightly said, it's firewood, that's all."

"Make it thirty-five," Rummins said.

"I *couldn't* sir, I *couldn't!* It's not worth it. And I simply mustn't allow myself to haggle[3] like this about a price. It's all wrong. I'll make you one final offer, and then I must go. Twenty pounds."

"I'll take it[4]," Rummins snapped[5]. "It's yours."

"Oh dear," Mr. Boggis said, clasping his hands. "There I go again. I should never have started this in the first place."

"You can't back out[6] now, Parson. A deal's a deal[7]."

"Yes, yes, I know."

"How're you going to take it?"

"Well, let me see. Perhaps if I were to drive my car up into the yard, you gentlemen would be kind enough to help me load it[8]?"

"In a car? This thing'll never go in a car! You'll need a truck for this!"

---

1 **the soles of his feet:** as solas dos seus pés • 2 **to give in:** desistir • 3 **to haggle:** pechinchar • 4 **I'll take it:** negócio fechado • 5 **snapped:** falou rispidamente • 6 **back out:** voltar atrás • 7 **a deal's a deal:** trato é trato • 8 **load it:** carregá-lo

"I don't think so. Anyway, we'll see. My car's on the road. I'll be back in a jiffy¹, We'll manage it somehow, I'm sure."

Mr. Boggis walked out into the yard and through the gate and then down the long track that led across the field towards the road. He found himself giggling² quite uncontrollably, and there was a feeling inside him as though hundreds and hundreds of tiny bubbles were rising up from his stomach and bursting merrily³ in the top of his head, like sparkling-water⁴. All the buttercups⁵ in the field were suddenly turning into golden sovereigns⁶, glistening⁷ in the sunlight. The ground was littered with them⁸, and he swung off the track⁹ on to the grass so that he could walk among them and tread on them¹⁰ and hear the little metallic tinkle¹¹ they made as he kicked them around with his toes. He was finding it difficult to stop himself from breaking into a run¹². But clergymen never run; they walk slowly. Walk slowly, Boggis. Keep calm, Boggis. There's no hurry¹³ now. The commode is yours! Yours for twenty pounds, and it's worth fifteen or twenty thousand! The Boggis Commode! In ten minutes it'll be loaded into your car—it'll go in easily—and you'll be driving back to London and singing all the way! Mr. Boggis driving the Boggis Commode home in the Boggis car.

---

1 **in a jiffy:** em um momento • 2 **giggling:** rindo • 3 **bursting merrily:** estourando alegremente • 4 **sparkling-water:** água com gás • 5 **buttercups:** botões-de-ouro • 6 **sovereigns:** moedas antigas que tinham o valor de uma libra • 7 **glistening:** brilhando • 8 **the ground was littered with them:** o chão estava coalhado deles • 9 **he swung off the track:** saiu do caminho • 10 **tread on them:** caminhar sobre eles • 11 **tinkle:** tilintar • 12 **breaking into a run:** sair correndo • 13 **there's no hurry:** não tem pressa

Historic occasion. What *wouldn't* a newspaperman[1] give to get a picture of that! Should he arrange[2] it? Perhaps he should. Wait and see. Oh, glorious day! Oh, lovely sunny summer day! Oh, glory be[3]!

Back in the farmhouse, Rummins was saying, "Fancy[4] that old bastard giving twenty pound for a load of junk like this."

"You did very nicely, Mr. Rummins," Claud told him. "You think he'll pay you?"

"We don't put it in the car till he do[5]."

"And what if it won't go in the car?" Claud asked. "You know what I think, Mr. Rummins? You want my honest opinion? I think the bloody thing's too big to go in the car. And then what happens? Then he's going to say to hell with it[6] and just drive off[7] without it and you'll never see him again. Nor the money either. He didn't seem all that keen on having it[8], you know."

Rummins paused to consider this new and rather alarming prospect.

"How can a thing like that possibly go in a car[9]?" Claud went on relentlessly[10]. "A parson never has a big car anyway. You ever seen[11] a parson with a big car, Mr. Rummins?"

"Can't say I have."

"Exactly! And now listen to me. I've got an idea. He told

---

1 **newspaperman:** jornalista • 2 **arrange:** preparar • 3 **oh, glory be!:** Aleluia! • 4 **fancy:** imaginem • 5 **till he do (until he does):** até que o faça • 6 **to hell with it:** ao diabo com isso • 7 **drive off:** fugir com o carro • 8 **all that keen on having it:** não estava tão animado em tê-la • 9 **go in a car:** caber em um carro • 10 **relentlessly:** implacavelmente • 11 **you ever seen (have you ever seen):** você já viu

us, didn't he, that it was only the legs he was wanting. Right? So all we've got to do is to cut 'em off quick right here on the spot[1] before he comes back, then it'll be sure to go in the car. All we're doing is saving him the trouble of cutting them off himself when he gets home. How about it Mr. Rummins?" Claud's flat bovine face glimmered with a mawkish pride[2].

"It's not such a bad idea at that" Rummins said, looking at the commode. "In fact it's a bloody good idea. Come on then, we'll have to hurry. You and Bert carry it out into the yard I'll get the saw[3]. Take the drawers out first."

Within a couple of minutes, Claud and Bert had carried the commode outside and had laid it upside down in the yard amidst the chicken droppings[4] and cow dung[5] and mud[6]. In the distance, half-way across the field they could see a small black figure striding[7] along the path towards the road. They paused to watch. There was something rather comical about the way in which this figure was conducting itself. Every now and again it would break into a trot[8] then it did a kind of hop[9], skip[10], and jump, and once it seemed as though the sound of a cheerful song came rippling[11] faintly to them from across the meadow[12].

"I reckon he's balmy[13]," Claud said and Bert grinned darkly, rolling his misty eye[14] slowly round in its socket[15].

---

1 **right here on the spot:** aqui mesmo • 2 **glimmered with mawkish pride:** iluminou com um orgulho repugnante • 3 **saw:** serra • 4 **amidst the chicken droppings:** entre os excrementos das galinhas • 5 **cow dung:** esterco das vacas • 6 **mud:** lama • 7 **striding:** caminhando a passos largos • 8 **break into a trot:** começava a trotar • 9 **hop:** salto • 10 **skip:** pulo • 11 **rippling:** como ondas • 12 **meadow:** pradaria • 13 **I reckon he's balmy:** eu acho que ele é doido • 14 **misty eye:** olho turvo • 15 **socket:** cavidade (órbita)

Rummins came waddling[1] over from the shed, squat[2] and froglike, carrying a long saw. Claud took the saw away from him and went to work.

"Cut' em close," Rummins said. "Don't forget he's going to use 'em on another table."

The mahogany was hard and very dry, and as Claud worked, a fine red dust sprayed out from the edge of the saw and fell softly to the ground. One by one, the legs came off, and when they were all severed[3], Bert stooped down[4] and arranged them carefully in a row[5].

Claud stepped back to survey the results of his labour. There was a longish pause.

"Just let me ask you one question, Mr. Rummins," he said slowly. "Even now, could *you* put that enormous thing into the back of a car?"

"Not unless it was a van[6]."

"Correct!" Claud cried. "And parsons don't have vans, you know. All they've got usually is piddling[7] little Morris Eights or Austin Sevens[8]."

"The legs is all he wants," Rummins said "If the rest of it won't go in, then he can leave it. He can't complain. He's got the legs."

"Now you know better'n that Mr. Rummins," Claud said patiently. "You know damn well he's going to start knocking the price[9] if he don't get every single bit of this into the car.

---

1 **waddling:** caminhando como um pato • 2 **squat:** atarracado • 3 **severed:** cortadas • 4 **stooped down:** agachou-se • 5 **in a row:** em uma fileira • 6 **van:** perua; van • 7 **piddling:** patéticos • 8 **Morris Eight, Austin Seven:** dois carros britânicos da época • 9 **knocking the price:** pechinchar o preço

A parson's just as cunning[1] as the rest of 'em when it comes to money, don't you make any mistake about that. Especially this old boy. So why don't we give him his firewood now and be done with it. Where d'you keep the axe[2]?"

"I reckon that's fair enough[3]" Rummins said "Bert, go fetch the axe."

Bert went into the shed and fetched a tall woodcutter's[4] axe and gave it to Claud. Claud spat[5] on the palms of his hands and rubbed them together[6]. Then, with a long-armed high-swinging action, he began fiercely attacking the legless carcass[7] of the commode.

It was hard work, and it took several minutes before he had the whole thing more or less smashed to pieces[8].

"I'll tell you one thing," he said, straightening up[9], wiping his brow[10]. "That was a bloody good carpenter put this job together[11] and I don't care what the parson says."

"We're just in time!" Rummins called out. "Here he comes!"

---

1 **cunning:** astuto • 2 **axe:** machado • 3 **that's fair enough:** está bem • 4 **woodcutter:** lenhador • 5 **spat:** cuspiu • 6 **rubbed them together:** esfregou uma na outra • 7 **the legless carcass:** a carcaça sem pernas • 8 **smashed to pieces:** feita em pedaços • 9 **straightening up:** colocando--se de pé • 10 **wiping his brow:** secando a sua testa • 11 **put this job together:** montar; juntar o negócio

# Edith Wharton
*The Other Two*

"A man would rather think that his wife has been brutalized by her first husband than that the process has been reversed."

BIOGRAFIA
**Edith Wharton**

Edith Wharton não é só a autora de *A era da inocência* (1921) – obra que lhe valeu o Pulitzer e o reconhecimento mundial. Ela ainda assinou outros 21 romances, 85 contos, alguns livros de viagens, três de poesia etc. Mas comecemos pelo princípio.

Edith Newbold Jones nasceu em 1862 em Nova York, no seio de uma família abastada, que abandonou com 23 anos para se casar com Edward Robbins Wharton, um homem rico, 12 anos mais velho que ela, pouco dado a ler livros, mas sim a festas sem hora para voltar para casa. Farta de suas muitas infidelidades (públicas), Edith conseguiu o divórcio em 1913, após 28 anos de casamento que quase a levaram a ser internada em um instituto psiquiátrico. (Uma crise nervosa a obrigou a ingressar no hospital após a última discussão.) Nas suas próprias palavras, "me casar foi o maior erro da minha vida". No fim do seu tumultuado casamento, Edith teve mais de uma aventura: a primeira, com um jornalista do *The Times* chamado William Fullerton; o romance mais longo, com a cantora de ópera Camilla Chabbert; e talvez o mais apaixonado, com a poeta Mercedes de Acosta.

Deixando de lado o tema amoroso, latente em toda sua obra, cabe dizer que Wharton escrevia desde criança, porém não publicou o seu primeiro romance até fazer 40 anos. Corria o ano de 1902 quando debutou com *The Valley of Decision*, romance claramente histórico. Três anos depois chegou a que é considerada a sua primeira grande obra, *The House of Mirth* (1905), uma sátira de ironia endiabrada sobre a sociedade aristocrática da época, da qual ela mesma era proveniente. Wharton era uma grande admiradora da Europa, o que a levou a cruzar o Atlântico 66 vezes antes de instalar-se definitivamente em Paris (por volta de 1911), deixando a sua casa, *The Mount*, que ela mesma havia projetado. A partir de 1919, alternaria sua residência entre as suas duas casas de campo, a *Pavilion Colombe*, perto de Saint-Brice-sous-Forêt, e o antigo convento de Sainte-Claire Le Château, em Hyères, no sudeste da França. Da época parisiense se destaca seu romance *Ethan Frome*, uma trágica história de amor ambientada na Nova Inglaterra publicada em 1911.

Wharton vivia na célebre Rue de Varenne, em Paris, quando estourou a Primeira Guerra Mundial. Graças aos seus contatos no governo francês, Wharton conseguiu permissão para viajar de motocicleta pelas linhas do *front*.

Ela descreve essa experiência em uma série de artigos que posteriormente foram compilados no ensaio *Fighting France: From Dunquerque to Belfort* (1915). Durante a guerra trabalhou para a Cruz Vermelha com os refugiados.

Wharton falava francês fluentemente e chegou a publicar indistintamente em inglês e em francês. Ela foi íntima de F. Scott Fitzgerald, Ernest Hemingway e Henry James. Não deixou de escrever enquanto viveu. Aliás, no seu leito de morte em Saint-Brice-sous-Forêt foram encontradas as últimas páginas do que seria seu próximo romance, *Os bucaneiros*. A história foi publicada tal qual em 1938 e, em 1993, foi reeditada e finalizada por Marion Mainwaring, após estudar as notas e sinopses da autora.

LAURA FERNÁNDEZ

APRESENTAÇÃO DO CONTO
**The Other Two**

Alice Waythorn é um mistério. Um mistério assíduo nos tribunais, um mistério que os advogados especialistas em litígios matrimoniais aguardam com uma xícara de café quente em seus escritórios. Casou três vezes e se divorciou duas, em uma época em que as mulheres não costumavam fazer essas coisas. Digamos que, naqueles tempos, as ruas de Nova York estavam ainda cheias de carruagens e uma pessoa divorciada (por duas vezes) era pouco mais que um sapato velho.

Quem diz isso é o próprio Waythorn, atual marido da senhora Alice, para quem sua própria esposa é um mistério.

Mas, por quê? Muito simples: após conhecer seu primeiro marido, um homem qualquer, pequeno e praticamente moribundo (tudo nele, do chapéu até os pés, parece puído), Waythorn se pergunta o que sua mulher deve ter visto nele. E por que teve uma filha com ele. Uma filha doente que o sr. Haskett (o primeiro marido) insiste em visitar uma vez por semana, tendo como consequência o encontro com o atual marido de sua ex-mulher. E o que dizer do segundo? O senhor Varick é um reconhecido homem de negócios que se vê envolvido em uma série de assuntos com Waythorn. E o que Waythorn vê nele?

Até que ponto pode-se conhecer uma pessoa através dos seus ex-maridos? O que cada um deles diz sobre ela?

Publicado inicialmente na revista Collert's e compilado na antologia *The Descent of Man and Other Stories*, editada em 1904, "The Other Two" é uma brilhante amostra do humor ácido da melhor amiga de Henry James (e que certamente, assim como ele, era fascinada por histórias de fantasmas).

Colocando a mulher no centro da ação, fato francamente provocador naquele momento, Wharton convertia o homem (neste caso os diversos homens) em pouco mais que um espectador do que acontecia com certeza na sala (salas sempre cheias, a aristocracia nos relatos de Edith Wharton está em todas as partes). Os encontros fortuitos, a condenação quase kafkiana do estoico senhor Waythorn (que não tem outra opção senão se dar bem com os "ex" de sua mulher), o caráter terrivelmente cômico do sempre sorridente senhor Varick (que parece se divertir com tudo o que acontece) e o mistério que rodeia a protagonista converteram esta história em uma versão em miniatura do microcosmo de Wharton: uma comédia de sociedade agridoce que gira em torno de um único eixo, a mulher.

Xícaras de chá, empregados, encontros de negócios, homens que tiveram que se mudar para Nova York seguindo a sua ex para poder desse jeito ver sua filha; o vocabulário de "The Other Two" se nutre de tudo aquilo que rodeia um homem de classe média alta da Nova York do início do século XX (não tem carros, e sim carruagens, e as senhoras pedem licença para se retirar).

Trata-se de uma época que a senhora Wharton vivenciou e na qual, assim como a protagonista, se divorciou e teve uma ou outra aventura que certamente a fizeram perguntar-se o quanto cada uma das suas conquistas dizia sobre ela.

LAURA FERNÁNDEZ

# The Other Two

I

WAYTHORN, ON THE DRAWING-ROOM HEARTH¹, waited for his wife to come down to dinner.

It was their first night under his own roof, and he was surprised at his thrill² of boyish agitation. He was not so old, to be sure—his glass³ gave him little more than the five-and-thirty years to which his wife confessed—but he had fancied himself⁴ already in the temperate zone; yet here he was listening for her step⁵ with a tender sense of all it symbolized, with some old trail of verse⁶ about the garlanded nuptial door-posts⁷ floating through his enjoyment of the pleasant room and the good dinner just beyond it.

They had been hastily recalled⁸ from their honeymoon by the illness of Lily Haskett, the child of Mrs. Waythorn's first marriage. The little girl, at Waythorn's desire, had been transferred to his house on the day of her mother's wedding, and the doctor, on their arrival, broke the news that she was ill with typhoid, but declared that all the symptoms were favorable. Lily could show twelve years of unblemished health⁹,

1 **hearth:** lareira • 2 **thrill:** arrepio; excitação • 3 **glass:** espelho • 4 **he had fancied himself:** tinha se imaginado • 5 **her step:** seu passo • 6 **some old trail of verse:** algum velho rastro de poesia • 7 **garlanded nuptial door-posts:** os batentes das portas decorados com guirlandas nupciais • 8 **they had been hastily recalled:** tiveram de voltar precipitadamente • 9 **unblemished health:** saúde de ferro

and the case promised to be a light one. The nurse spoke as reassuringly[1], and after a moment of alarm Mrs. Waythorn had adjusted herself to the situation. She was very fond of Lily[2]—her affection for the child had perhaps been her decisive charm[3] in Waythorn's eyes—but she had the perfectly balanced nerves which her little girl had inherited, and no woman ever wasted less tissue[4] in unproductive worry. Waythorn was therefore[5] quite prepared to see her come in presently, a little late because of a last look at Lily, but as serene and well-appointed[6] as if her good-night kiss had been laid on the brow[7] of health. Her composure was restful to him[8]; it acted as ballast to[9] his somewhat unstable sensibilities. As he pictured her bending over the child's bed[10] he thought how soothing[11] her presence must be in illness: her very step would prognosticate recovery.

His own life had been a gray one, from temperament rather than circumstance, and he had been drawn to her by the unperturbed gayety[12] which kept her fresh and elastic at an age when most women's activities are growing either slack[13] or febrile. He knew what was said about her; for, popular as she was, there had always been a faint undercurrent of detraction[14]. When she had appeared in New York, nine or ten

---

1 **reassuringly:** de modo tranquilizador • 2 **she was very fond of Lily:** ela tinha muito carinho por Lily • 3 **charm:** encanto; atrativo • 4 **tissue:** lenço • 5 **therefore:** portanto • 6 **well-appointed:** bem preparada • 7 **brow:** testa; fronte • 8 **her composure was restful to him:** a sua serenidade lhe fazia bem • 9 **it acted as ballast to:** funcionava como um lastro • 10 **as he pictured her bending over the child's bed:** ao imaginá-la inclinada sobre a cama da criança • 11 **soothing:** tranquilizadora • 12 **gayety (gaiety):** alegria • 13 **slack:** lenta; sem energia • 14 **a faint undercurrent of detraction:** uma leve corrente de maledicência

years earlier, as the pretty Mrs. Haskett whom Gus Varick had unearthed[1] somewhere—was it in Pittsburgh or Utica? —society, while promptly[2] accepting her, had reserved the right to cast a doubt on its own discrimination[3]. Inquiry[4], however, established her undoubted connection with a socially reigning family, and explained her recent divorce as the natural result of a runaway match[5] at seventeen; and as nothing was known of Mr. Haskett it was easy to believe the worst of him.

Alice Haskett's remarriage with Gus Varick was a passport to the set[6] whose recognition she coveted[7], and for a few years the Varicks were the most popular couple in town. Unfortunately the alliance was brief and stormy[8], and this time the husband had his champions[9]. Still[10], even Varick's stanchest[11] supporters admitted that he was not meant for matrimony, and Mrs. Varick's grievances[12] were of a nature to bear the inspection of the New York courts[13]. A New York divorce is in itself a diploma of virtue, and in the semi-widowhood[14] of this second separation Mrs. Varick took on an air of sanctity, and was allowed to confide her wrongs[15] to some of the most scrupulous ears in town. But when it was known that she was to marry Waythorn there was a momentary reaction.

---

1 **unearthed:** descoberto • 2 **promptly:** de imediato • 3 **to cast a doubt on its own discrimination:** pôr em dúvida seu próprio discernimento • 4 **inquiry:** investigações • 5 **a runaway match:** um casamento precipitado • 6 **set:** círculo social • 7 **she coveted:** ela cobiçava • 8 **stormy:** tempestuosa • 9 **champions:** defensores • 10 **still:** ainda assim; no entanto • 11 **stanchest (staunchest):** aguerridos • 12 **grievances:** queixas • 13 **courts:** tribunais • 14 **widowhood:** viuvez • 15 **to confide her wrongs:** confidenciar seus erros

Her best friends would have preferred to see her remain in the role of the injured wife[1], which was as becoming[2] to her as crape to a rosy complexion[3]. True, a decent time had elapsed, and it was not even suggested that Waythorn had supplanted his predecessor. Still, people shook their heads over him, and one grudging friend[4], to whom he affirmed that he took the step with his eyes open, replied oracularly: "Yes—and with your ears shut."

Waythorn could afford to smile at these innuendoes[5]. In the Wall Street phrase, he had "discounted" them[6]. He knew that society has not yet adapted itself to the consequences of divorce, and that till the adaptation takes place every woman who uses the freedom the law accords her must be her own social justification. Waythorn had an amused confidence in his wife's ability to justify herself. His expectations were fulfilled[7], and before the wedding took place Alice Varick's group had rallied openly to her support[8]. She took it all imperturbably: she had a way of surmounting obstacles without seeming to be aware of them, and Waythorn looked back with wonder at the trivialities over which he had worn his nerves thin[9]. He had the sense of having found refuge in a richer, warmer nature than his own, and his satisfaction, at the moment, was humorously summed up[10] in the thought

---

1 **the injured wife:** a esposa ferida • 2 **becoming:** apropriado • 3 **as crape to a rosy complexion:** como crepe para uma tez rósea • 4 **one grudging friend:** um amigo com má vontade • 5 **innuendos:** indiretas; insinuações • 6 **he had discounted them:** ele as tinha descontado • 7 **his expectations were fulfilled:** as suas expectativas foram atendidas • 8 **had rallied ... to her support:** se uniu... para apoiá-la • 9 **he had worn his nerves thin:** ele tinha esgotado sua paciência • 10 **summed up:** resumia-se

that his wife, when she had done all she could for Lily, would not be ashamed¹ to come down and enjoy a good dinner.

The anticipation of such enjoyment was not, however, the sentiment expressed by Mrs. Waythorn's charming face when she presently joined him. Though she had put on her most engaging teagown² she had neglected³ to assume the smile that went with it, and Waythorn thought he had never seen her look so nearly worried.

"What is it?" he asked. "Is anything wrong with Lily?"

"No; I've just been in and she's still sleeping." Mrs. Waythorn hesitated. "But something tiresome⁴ has happened."

He had taken her two hands, and now perceived that she was crushing a paper⁵ between them.

"This letter?"

"Yes—Mr. Haskett has written—I mean his lawyer has written."

Waythorn felt himself flush⁶ uncomfortably. He dropped his wife's hands.

"What about?"

"About seeing Lily. You know the courts—"

"Yes, yes," he interrupted nervously.

Nothing was known about Haskett in New York. He was vaguely supposed to have remained in the outer⁷ darkness from which his wife had been rescued, and Waythorn was one of the few who were aware that he had given up his

---

1 **would not be ashamed:** não se acanharia • 2 **though she had put on her most engaging teagown:** apesar de ela estar usando seu vestido mais atraente • 3 **she had neglected:** ela tinha deixado de lado • 4 **tiresome:** um fato aborrecedor • 5 **she was crushing a paper:** ela segurava um papel amassado • 6 **felt himself flush:** sentiu que ficava vermelho • 7 **outer:** externa

business in Utica and followed her to New York in order to be near his little girl. In the days of his wooing[1], Waythorn had often met Lily on the doorstep, rosy and smiling, on her way "to see papa."

"I am so sorry," Mrs. Waythorn murmured.

He roused himself[2]. "What does he want?"

"He wants to see her. You know she goes to him once a week."

"Well—he doesn't expect her to go to him now, does he?"

"No—he has heard of her illness; but he expects to come here."

"Here?"

Mrs. Waythorn reddened under his gaze[3]. They looked away from each other.

"I'm afraid he has the right.... You'll see...." She made a proffer of the letter[4].

Waythorn moved away with a gesture of refusal[5]. He stood staring about the softly lighted room, which a moment before had seemed so full of bridal intimacy[6].

"I'm so sorry," she repeated. "If Lily could have been moved—"

"That's out of the question[7]," he returned impatiently.

"I suppose so."

---

1 **wooing:** cortejo • 2 **he roused himself:** ele se levantou • 3 **reddened under his gaze:** se ruborizou diante do seu olhar • 4 **she made a proffer of the letter:** ela lhe entregou a carta • 5 **refusal:** recusa • 6 **bridal intimacy:** intimidade conjugal • 7 **that's out of the question:** isto está fora de questão

Her lip was beginning to tremble, and he felt himself a brute[1].

"He must come, of course," he said. "When is—his day?"

"I'm afraid—to-morrow."

"Very well. Send a note in the morning."

The butler[2] entered to announce dinner.

Waythorn turned to his wife. "Come—you must be tired. It's beastly[3], but try to forget about it," he said, drawing her hand through his arm[4].

"You're so good, dear. I'll try," she whispered back.

Her face cleared at once[5], and as she looked at him across the flowers, between the rosy candle-shades[6], he saw her lips waver back into a smile[7].

"How pretty everything is!" she sighed luxuriously[8].

He turned to the butler. "The champagne at once, please. Mrs. Waythorn is tired."

In a moment or two their eyes met above the sparkling glasses[9]. Her own were quite clear and untroubled[10]: he saw that she had obeyed his injunction[11] and forgotten.

---

1 **he felt himself a brute:** sentiu ter se comportado como um animal • 2 **butler:** mordomo • 3 **it's beastly:** é desagradável • 4 **drawing her hand through his arm:** entrelaçando sua mão no braço dele • 5 **her face cleared at once:** seu rosto se descontraiu de uma vez • 6 **candle-shades:** sombra das velas • 7 **he saw her lips waver back into a smile:** viu que seus lábios voltavam a esboçar um sorriso • 8 **she sighed luxuriously:** ela suspirou copiosamente • 9 **sparkling glasses:** taças espumantes • 10 **untroubled (eyes):** olhar tranquilo • 11 **injunction:** ordem

## II

Waythorn, the next morning, went downtown earlier than usual. Haskett was not likely to come till the afternoon, but the instinct of flight drove him forth[1]. He meant to stay away all day—he had thoughts of dining at his club. As his door closed behind him he reflected[2] that before he opened it again it would have admitted another man who had as much right to enter it as himself, and the thought filled him with a physical repugnance.

He caught the "elevated[3]" at the employees' hour, and found himself crushed between two layers of pendulous humanity[4]. At Eighth Street the man facing him wriggled out[5] and another took his place. Waythorn glanced up and saw that it was Gus Varick. The men were so close together that it was impossible to ignore the smile of recognition on Varick's handsome overblown[6] face. And after all—why not? They had always been on good terms, and Varick had been divorced before Waythorn's attentions to his wife began. The two exchanged a word on the perennial grievance of the congested trains, and when a seat at their side was miraculously left empty the instinct of self-preservation made Waythorn slip into it after Varick.

The latter drew the stout man's breath of relief[7].

1 **the instinct of flight drove him forth:** o instinto de fugir tomou conta dele • 2 **he reflected:** ele refletiu • 3 **elevated (elevated railroad):** ferrovia urbana elevada • 4 **crushed between two layers of pendulous humanity:** prensado entre duas camadas de humanidade oscilante • 5 **wriggled out:** saiu ziguezagueando por entre as pessoas • 6 **overblown:** presunçosa • 7 **the latter drew the stout man's breath of relief:** este último deu um suspiro de alívio próprio de um homem corpulento

"Lord—I was beginning to feel like a pressed flower." He leaned back, looking unconcernedly at Waythorn. "Sorry to hear that Sellers is knocked out[1] again."

"Sellers?" echoed Waythorn, starting at his partner's name[2].

Varick looked surprised. "You didn't know he was laid up with the gout[3]?"

"No. I've been away—I only got back last night." Waythorn felt himself reddening in anticipation of the other's smile.

"Ah—yes; to be sure. And Sellers's attack came on two days ago. I'm afraid he's pretty bad. Very awkward for me, as it happens, because he was just putting through a rather important thing for me."

"Ah?" Waythorn wondered vaguely since when Varick had been dealing in "important things." Hitherto[4] he had dabbled only in the shallow pools of speculation[5], with which Waythorn's office did not usually concern itself.

It occurred to him that Varick might be talking at random[6], to relieve the strain of their propinquity[7]. That strain was becoming momentarily more apparent to Waythorn, and when, at Cortlandt Street[8], he caught sight of an

---

1 **Sellers is knocked out:** Sellers ficou doente • 2 **starting at his partner's name:** estranhando ouvir o nome do seu sócio • 3 **he was laid up with the gout:** estava de cama, com gota • 4 **hitherto:** até agora • 5 **he had dabbled only in the shallow pools of speculation:** só tinha mergulhado nas águas rasas da especulação • 6 **talking at random:** falando por falar • 7 **to relieve the strain of their propinquity:** para diminuir a tensão provocada pela sua proximidade • 8 **Cortlandt Street:** rua e estação situadas na zona sul de Manhattan

acquaintance, and had a sudden vision of the picture he and Varick must present to an initiated eye, he jumped up with a muttered excuse[1].

"I hope you'll find Sellers better," said Varick civilly[2], and he stammered back[3]: "If I can be of any use to you—" and let the departing crowd sweep him to[4] the platform.

At his office he heard that Sellers was in fact ill with the gout, and would probably not be able to leave the house for some weeks.

"I'm sorry it should have happened so, Mr. Waythorn," the senior clerk said with affable significance. "Mr. Sellers was very much upset[5] at the idea of giving you such a lot of extra work just now."

"Oh, that's no matter," said Waythorn hastily. He secretly welcomed the pressure of additional business, and was glad to think that, when the day's work was over, he would have to call at his partner's[6] on the way home.

He was late for luncheon[7], and turned in at the nearest restaurant instead of going to his club. The place was full, and the waiter hurried him to the back of the room to capture the only vacant table. In the cloud of cigar-smoke Waythorn did not at once distinguish his neighbors; but presently[8], looking about him[9], he saw Varick seated a few feet off. This time, luckily, they were too far apart for conversation, and

---

1 **he jumped up with a muttered excuse:** levantou-se de repente murmurando uma desculpa • 2 **civilly:** educadamente • 3 **he stammered back:** ele respondeu gaguejando • 4 **let the departing crowd sweep him to:** deixou a multidão empurrá-lo até • 5 **upset:** contrariado; desapontado • 6 **he would have to call at his partner's:** ele teria de visitar seu sócio • 7 **luncheon:** almoço; lanche • 8 **presently:** logo; em seguida • 9 **looking about him:** olhando ao seu redor

Varick, who faced another way[1], had probably not even seen him; but there was an irony in their renewed nearness.

Varick was said to be fond of good living, and as Waythorn sat despatching his hurried luncheon he looked across half enviously at the other's leisurely[2] degustation of his meal. When Waythorn first saw him he had been helping himself[3] with critical deliberation to a bit of Camembert at the ideal point of liquefaction, and now, the cheese removed, he was just pouring his cafe[4] double from its little two-storied earthen pot[5]. He poured slowly, his ruddy[6] profile bent above the task, and one beringed[7] white hand steadying the lid of the coffee-pot; then he stretched his other hand to the decanter[8] of cognac at his elbow, filled a liqueur-glass, took a tentative sip[9], and poured the brandy into his coffee-cup.

Waythorn watched him in a kind of fascination. What was he thinking of—only of the flavor of the coffee and the liqueur? Had the morning's meeting left no more trace in his thoughts than on his face? Had his wife so completely passed out of his life that even this odd[10] encounter with her present husband, within a week after her remarriage, was no more than an incident in his day? And as Waythorn mused[11], another idea struck him: had Haskett ever met Varick as Varick and he had just met? The recollection[12] of Haskett perturbed him, and he rose and left the restaurant, taking

---

1 **who faced another way:** que estava voltado para outro lado • 2 **leisurely:** vagarosamente • 3 **he had been helping himself:** ele estava se servindo • 4 **he was just pouring his cafe:** ele estava servindo seu café • 5 **two-storied earthen pot:** cafeteira de barro de dois andares • 6 **ruddy:** corado • 7 **beringed:** com anel no dedo • 8 **decanter:** garrafa • 9 **took a tentative sip:** provou um gole • 10 **odd:** estranho • 11 **mused:** refletia • 12 **recollection:** lembrança

a circuitous way out¹ to escape the placid irony of Varick's nod.

It was after seven when Waythorn reached home. He thought the footman² who opened the door looked at him oddly.

"How is Miss Lily?" he asked in haste³.

"Doing very well, sir. A gentleman—"

"Tell Barlow to put off dinner⁴ for half an hour," Waythorn cut him off⁵, hurrying upstairs.

He went straight to his room and dressed without seeing his wife. When he reached the drawing-room she was there, fresh and radiant. Lily's day had been good; the doctor was not coming back that evening.

At dinner Waythorn told her of Sellers's illness and of the resulting complications. She listened sympathetically⁶, adjuring him not to let himself be overworked, and asking vague feminine questions about the routine of the office. Then she gave him the chronicle of Lily's day; quoted⁷ the nurse and doctor, and told him who had called to inquire. He had never seen her more serene and unruffled⁸. It struck him⁹, with a curious pang¹⁰, that she was very happy in being with him, so happy that she found a childish pleasure in rehearsing¹¹ the trivial incidents of her day.

---

1 **taking a circuitous way out:** fazendo uma volta para sair • 2 **footman:** o criado • 3 **he asked in haste:** perguntou apressado • 4 **to put off dinner:** atrasar o jantar (a ceia) • 5 **cut him off:** o interrompeu • 6 **she listened sympathetically:** ela escutou compreensivamente • 7 **quoted:** citou • 8 **unruffled:** calma • 9 **it struck him:** ficou impressionado • 10 **a curious pang:** uma pontada curiosa • 11 **in rehearsing:** em reproduzir

After dinner they went to the library, and the servant put the coffee and liqueurs on a low table before her and left the room. She looked singularly soft and girlish in her rosy pale dress, against the dark leather of one of his bachelor armchairs[1]. A day earlier the contrast would have charmed him.

He turned away now, choosing a cigar with affected deliberation.

"Did Haskett come?" he asked, with his back to her[2].

"Oh, yes—he came."

"You didn't see him, of course?"

She hesitated a moment. "I let the nurse see him[3]."

That was all. There was nothing more to ask. He swung round toward her, applying a match to his cigar. Well, the thing was over for a week[4], at any rate[5]. He would try not to think of it. She looked up at him, a trifle rosier than usual[6], with a smile in her eyes.

"Ready for your coffee, dear?"

He leaned against the mantelpiece[7], watching her as she lifted the coffee-pot. The lamplight struck a gleam[8] from her bracelets and tipped her soft hair with brightness[9]. How light and slender she was, and how each gesture flowed into the next! She seemed a creature all compact of harmonies. As the thought of Haskett receded, Waythorn felt himself yielding

---

1 **bachelor armchairs:** poltronas • 2 **with his back to her:** de costas para ela • 3 **I let the nurse see him:** deixei que a enfermeira o visse • 4 **the thing was over for a week:** o assunto seria deixado de lado por uma semana • 5 **at any rate:** pelo menos • 6 **a trifle rosier than usual:** um pouco mais ruborizada que de costume • 7 **he leaned against the mantelpiece:** encostou na estante da lareira • 8 **gleam:** raio luminoso; clarão • 9 **tipped her soft hair with brightness:** derramou brilho em seu cabelo suave

again to[1] the joy of possessorship. They were his, those white hands with their flitting motions[2], his the light haze of hair, the lips and eyes. . . .

She set down the coffee-pot, and reaching for the decanter of cognac, measured off a liqueur-glass and poured it into his cup.

Waythorn uttered[3] a sudden exclamation.

"What is the matter?" she said, startled.

"Nothing; only—I don't take cognac in my coffee."

"Oh, how stupid of me," she cried.

Their eyes met, and she blushed a sudden agonized red.

### III

Ten days later, Mr. Sellers, still house-bound[4], asked Waythorn to call on his way downtown.

The senior partner, with his swaddled foot propped up by the fire[5], greeted his associate with an air of embarrassment[6].

"I'm sorry, my dear fellow; I've got to ask you to do an awkward thing for me."

Waythorn waited, and the other went on, after a pause apparently given to the arrangement of his phrases: "The

---

1 **yielding again to:** se render novamente • 2 **flitting motions:** movimentos rápidos • 3 **uttered:** proferiu; emitiu • 4 **house-bound:** confinado em casa • 5 **with his swaddled foot propped up by the fire:** com seu pé enfaixado levantado próximo à lareira • 6 **embarrassment:** vergonha

fact is, when I was knocked out I had just gone into a rather complicated piece of business for—Gus Varick."

"Well?" said Waythorn, with an attempt to put him at his ease¹.

"Well—it's this way: Varick came to me the day before my attack. He had evidently had an inside tip² from somebody, and had made about a hundred thousand. He came to me for advice, and I suggested his going in with Vanderlyn³."

"Oh, the deuce⁴!" Waythorn exclaimed. He saw in a flash what had happened. The investment was an alluring⁵ one, but required negotiation. He listened intently while Sellers put the case before him⁶, and, the statement ended, he said: "You think I ought to see Varick?"

"I'm afraid I can't as yet⁷. The doctor is obdurate⁸. And this thing can't wait. I hate to ask you, but no one else in the office knows the ins and outs⁹ of it."

Waythorn stood silent. He did not care a farthing¹⁰ for the success of Varick's venture¹¹, but the honor of the office was to be considered, and he could hardly refuse to oblige¹² his partner.

"Very well," he said, "I'll do it."

---

1 **with an attempt to put him at his ease:** tentando deixá-lo à vontade • 2 **inside tip:** palpite de quem está por dentro • 3 **I suggested his going in with Vanderlyn:** sugeri que se consulte com Vanderlyn • 4 **oh, the deuce!:** Ó céus! • 5 **alluring:** tentador • 6 **put the case before him:** apresentou-lhe o caso • 7 **as yet:** ainda • 8 **obdurate:** obstinado • 9 **the ins and outs:** os detalhes; pormenores • 10 **he did not care a farthing:** não estava nem aí • 11 **venture:** operação; empreendimento • 12 **to oblige:** agradar

That afternoon, apprised[1] by telephone, Varick called at the office. Waythorn, waiting in his private room, wondered what the others thought of it. The newspapers, at the time of Mrs. Waythorn's marriage, had acquainted[2] their readers with every detail of her previous matrimonial ventures, and Waythorn could fancy[3] the clerks smiling behind Varick's back as he was ushered in[4].

Varick bore himself[5] admirably. He was easy without being undignified[6], and Waythorn was conscious of cutting a much less impressive figure[7]. Varick had no head for business, and the talk prolonged itself for nearly an hour while Waythorn set forth[8] with scrupulous precision the details of the proposed transaction.

"I'm awfully obliged to you[9]," Varick said as he rose. "The fact is I'm not used to having much money to look after, and I don't want to make an ass of myself[10]—" He smiled, and Waythorn could not help noticing that[11] there was something pleasant about his smile. "It feels uncommonly queer[12] to have enough cash to pay one's bills. I'd have sold my soul for it a few years ago!"

---

1 **apprised:** avisado • 2 **had acquainted:** tinham informado • 3 **could fancy:** podia imaginar • 4 **as he was ushered in:** enquanto ele era introduzido na sala • 5 **bore himself:** se comportou • 6 **he was easy without being undignified:** foi naturalmente descontraído sem deixar de ser educado • 7 **was conscious of cutting a much less impressive figure:** estava consciente de passar uma imagem muito menos imponente • 8 **set forth:** fez a exposição • 9 **I'm awfully obliged to you:** eu lhe sou infinitamente grato • 10 **I don't want to make an ass of myself:** não quero fazer papel de burro • 11 **could not help noticing that:** não pôde deixar de notar que • 12 **queer:** estranho

Waythorn winced[1] at the allusion. He had heard it rumored that a lack of funds had been one of the determining causes of the Varick separation, but it did not occur to him that Varick's words were intentional. It seemed more likely that the desire to keep clear of embarrassing[2] topics had fatally drawn him into[3] one. Waythorn did not wish to be outdone in civility[4].

"We'll do the best[5] we can for you," he said. "I think this is a good thing you're in."

"Oh, I'm sure it's immense. It's awfully good of you—" Varick broke off[6], embarrassed. "I suppose the thing's settled now—but if—"

"If anything happens before Sellers is about[7], I'll see you again," said Waythorn quietly. He was glad, in the end, to appear the more self-possessed[8] of the two.

The course of Lily's illness ran smooth[9], and as the days passed Waythorn grew used to the idea of Haskett's weekly visit. The first time the day came round, he stayed out late, and questioned his wife as to the visit on his return. She replied at once that Haskett had merely seen the nurse downstairs, as the doctor did not wish any one in the child's sickroom till after the crisis.

---

1 **winced:** estremeceu • 2 **to keep clear of embarrassing topics:** evitar temas embaraçosos • 3 **had ... drawn him into:** o levaram a • 4 **to be outdone in civility:** se exceder em civilidades • 5 **we'll do our best:** faremos o melhor possível • 6 **broke off:** interrompeu-se • 7 **before Sellers is about:** antes que Sellers volte • 8 **self-possessed:** contido; dono de si • 9 **ran smooth:** correu tranquilo

The following week Waythorn was again conscious of the recurrence of the day[1], but had forgotten it by the time he came home to dinner. The crisis of the disease came a few days later, with a rapid decline of fever, and the little girl was pronounced out of danger. In the rejoicing which ensued[2] the thought of Haskett passed out of Waythorn's mind and one afternoon, letting himself into the house with a latch-key[3], he went straight to his library without noticing a shabby[4] hat and umbrella in the hall.

In the library he found a small effaced-looking man[5] with a thinnish gray beard sitting on the edge of a chair. The stranger might have been a piano-tuner[6], or one of those mysteriously efficient persons who are summoned[7] in emergencies to adjust some detail of the domestic machinery. He blinked[8] at Waythorn through a pair of gold-rimmed spectacles and said mildly[9]: "Mr. Waythorn, I presume? I am Lily's father."

Waythorn flushed. "Oh—" he stammered[10] uncomfortably. He broke off, disliking to appear rude. Inwardly[11] he was trying to adjust the actual Haskett to the image of him projected by his wife's reminiscences. Waythorn had been allowed to infer that Alice's first husband was a brute.

---

1 **the recurrence of the day:** do acontecido durante o dia • 2 **in the rejoicing which ensued:** com a alegria que se sucedeu • 3 **latchkey:** chave • 4 **shabby:** puído; surrado; desgastado • 5 **effaced-looking man:** um homem apagado, retraído • 6 **piano-tuner:** afinador de piano • 7 **who are summoned:** que são convocados • 8 **he blinked:** ele piscou • 9 **mildly:** gentilmente; suavemente • 10 **he stammered:** gaguejou • 11 **inwardly:** no seu íntimo

# THE OTHER TWO

"I am sorry to intrude[1]," said Haskett, with his over-the-counter politeness[2].

"Don't mention it," returned Waythorn, collecting himself[3]. "I suppose the nurse has been told?"

"I presume so. I can wait," said Haskett. He had a resigned way of speaking, as though life had worn down[4] his natural powers of resistance.

Waythorn stood on the threshold[5], nervously pulling off his gloves.

"I'm sorry you've been detained[6]. I will send for the nurse," he said; and as he opened the door he added with an effort: "I'm glad we can give you a good report of Lily." He winced as the we slipped out[7], but Haskett seemed not to notice it.

"Thank you, Mr. Waythorn. It's been an anxious time for me."

"Ah, well, that's past. Soon she'll be able to go to you." Waythorn nodded and passed out[8].

In his own room, he flung himself down with a groan[9]. He hated the womanish sensibility which made him suffer so acutely from the grotesque chances of life[10]. He had known when he married that his wife's former husbands were both living, and that amid the multiplied contacts of modern

---

1 **to intrude:** importunar • 2 **over-the-counter politeness:** gentileza além da conta • 3 **collecting himself:** se recompondo • 4 **had worn down:** tivesse abalado • 5 **threshold:** soleira • 6 **I'm sorry you've been detained:** lamento que o fizeram esperar • 7 **slipped out:** escapou • 8 **passed out:** saiu • 9 **he flung himself down with a groan:** se deixou cair com um gemido • 10 **the grotesque chances of life:** acasos grotescos da vida

existence there were a thousand chances to one[1] that he would run against one or the other, yet he found himself as much disturbed by his brief encounter with Haskett as though the law had not obligingly removed all difficulties in the way of their meeting.

Waythorn sprang up[2] and began to pace the room nervously. He had not suffered half so much from his two meetings with Varick. It was Haskett's presence in his own house that made the situation so intolerable. He stood still, hearing steps in the passage.

"This way, please," he heard the nurse say. Haskett was being taken upstairs, then: not a corner of the house but was open to him. Waythorn dropped into another chair[3], staring vaguely ahead of him. On his dressing-table stood a photograph of Alice, taken when he had first known her. She was Alice Varick then—how fine and exquisite he had thought her! Those were Varick's pearls about her neck. At Waythorn's instance[4] they had been returned before her marriage. Had Haskett ever given her any trinkets[5]—and what had become of them, Waythorn wondered? He realized suddenly that he knew very little of Haskett's past or present situation; but from the man's appearance and manner of speech he could reconstruct with curious precision the surroundings of Alice's first marriage. And it startled him[6] to think that she had, in the background of her life, a phase of existence so

---

1 **a thousand chances to one:** mil chances em uma • 2 **sprang up:** ficou em pé em um pulo • 3 **dropped into another chair:** se jogou em outra cadeira • 4 **at Waythorn's instance:** sob insistência de Waythorn • 5 **trinkets:** joias sem valor • 6 **it startled him:** o surpreendeu

different from anything with which he had connected her. Varick, whatever his faults[1], was a gentleman, in the conventional, traditional sense of the term: the sense which at that moment seemed, oddly enough, to have most meaning to Waythorn. He and Varick had the same social habits, spoke the same language, understood the same allusions. But this other man . . . it was grotesquely uppermost[2] in Waythorn's mind that Haskett had worn a made-up tie[3] attached with an elastic. Why should that ridiculous detail symbolize the whole man? Waythorn was exasperated by his own paltriness[4], but the fact of the tie expanded, forced itself on him[5], became as it were the key to Alice's past. He could see her, as Mrs. Haskett, sitting in a "front parlor[6]" furnished in plush[7], with a pianola, and a copy of "Ben Hur" on the centre-table. He could see her going to the theatre with Haskett—or perhaps even to a "Church Sociable[8]"—she in a "picture hat[9]" and Haskett in a black frock-coat[10], a little creased[11], with the made-up tie on an elastic. On the way home they would stop and look at the illuminated shop-windows, lingering over[12] the photographs of New York actresses. On Sunday afternoons Haskett would take her for a walk, pushing Lily ahead of them in a white enameled perambulator[13], and Waythorn had a vision of the people they would stop and talk to. He

---

1 **whatever his faults:** sejam quais fossem seus defeitos • 2 **uppermost:** predominante • 3 **made-up tie:** gravata de laço pronto • 4 **paltriness:** mesquinharia • 5 **forced itself on him:** se impôs • 6 **front parlor:** sala de estar • 7 **in plush:** felpudos • 8 **Church Sociable:** reunião social da igreja • 9 **picture hat:** chapéu de aba larga • 10 **frock-coat:** sobrecasaca • 11 **creased:** enrugado • 12 **lingering over:** detendo-se sobre • 13 **enameled perambulator:** carrinho de criança envernizado

could fancy how pretty Alice must have looked, in a dress adroitly[1] constructed from the hints[2] of a New York fashion-paper[3]; how she must have looked down on the other women, chafing at her life[4], and secretly feeling that she belonged in a bigger place.

For the moment his foremost[5] thought was one of wonder at the way in which she had shed the phase of existence which her marriage with Haskett implied. It was as if her whole aspect, every gesture, every inflection, every allusion, were a studied negation of that period of her life. If she had denied being married to Haskett she could hardly have stood more convicted of duplicity than in this obliteration[6] of the self which had been his wife.

Waythorn started up, checking himself in the analysis of her motives. What right had he to create a fantastic effigy of her and then pass judgment on it[7]? She had spoken vaguely of her first marriage as unhappy, had hinted[8], with becoming reticence, that Haskett had wrought havoc among her young illusions[9]. . . . It was a pity for Waythorn's peace of mind that Haskett's very inoffensiveness shed a new light[10] on the nature of those illusions. A man would rather think that his wife has been brutalized by her first husband than that the process has been reversed.

---

1 **adroitly:** habilmente • 2 **the hints:** as sugestões • 3 **fashion-paper:** revista de moda • 4 **chafing at her life:** irritada com a vida que levava • 5 **foremost:** primeiro • 6 **obliteration:** destruição • 7 **pass judgment on it:** julgá-la • 8 **had hinted:** tinha insinuado • 9 **had wrought havoc among her young illusions:** tinha jogado por terra suas ilusões juvenis • 10 **shed a new light:** jogou uma nova luz

## IV

"Mr Waythorn, I don't like that French governess[1] of Lily's."

Haskett, subdued and apologetic[2], stood before Waythorn in the library, revolving his shabby hat in his hand[3].

Waythorn, surprised in his armchair over the evening paper, stared back perplexedly at his visitor.

"You'll excuse my asking to see you," Haskett continued. "But this is my last visit, and I thought if I could have a word with you it would be a better way than writing to Mrs. Waythorn's lawyer."

Waythorn rose uneasily[4]. He did not like the French governess either; but that was irrelevant.

"I am not so sure of that," he returned stiffly[5]; "but since you wish it I will give your message to—my wife." He always hesitated over the possessive pronoun in addressing Haskett.

The latter sighed. "I don't know as that will help much. She didn't like it when I spoke to her."

Waythorn turned red. "When did you see her?" he asked.

"Not since the first day I came to see Lily—right after she was taken sick. I remarked to her then that I didn't like the governess."

Waythorn made no answer. He remembered distinctly that, after that first visit, he had asked his wife if she had seen Haskett. She had lied to him then, but she had respected

---

1 **governess:** governanta; professora • 2 **subdued and apologetic:** contido e com ar de desculpa • 3 **revolving his shabby hat in his hand:** fazendo girar seu chapéu surrado entre as mãos • 4 **uneasily:** inquieto • 5 **he returned stiffly:** replicou bruscamente

his wishes since; and the incident cast a curious light on her character. He was sure she would not have seen Haskett that first day if she had divined that Waythorn would object, and the fact that she did not divine it was almost as disagreeable to the latter as the discovery that she had lied to him.

"I don't like the woman," Haskett was repeating with mild[1] persistency. "She ain't straight[2], Mr. Waythorn—she'll teach the child to be underhand[3]. I've noticed a change in Lily—she's too anxious to please[4]—and she don't always tell the truth. She used to be the straightest child, Mr. Waythorn —" He broke off, his voice a little thick. "Not but what I want her to have a stylish education," he ended.

Waythorn was touched. "I'm sorry, Mr. Haskett; but frankly, I don't quite see what I can do."

Haskett hesitated. Then he laid his hat on the table, and advanced to the hearth-rug[5], on which Waythorn was standing. There was nothing aggressive in his manner; but he had the solemnity of a timid man resolved on a decisive measure.

"There's just one thing you can do, Mr. Waythorn," he said. "You can remind Mrs. Waythorn that, by the decree of the courts, I am entitled[6] to have a voice in Lily's bringing up[7]." He paused, and went on more deprecatingly[8]: "I'm not the kind to talk about enforcing my rights[9], Mr. Waythorn.

---

1 **mild:** leve • 2 **she ain't (she is not) straight:** ela não é confiável • 3 **underhand:** dissimulada • 4 **too anxious to please:** muito ansiosa por agradar • 5 **hearth-rug:** tapete da lareira • 6 **I am entitled:** estou autorizado • 7 **bringing up:** educação • 8 **went on more deprecatingly:** prosseguiu com tom de reprovação maior • 9 **I'm not the kind to talk about enforcing my rights:** não sou do tipo que fala sobre impor meus direitos

I don't know as I think a man is entitled to rights he hasn't known how to hold on to[1]; but this business of the child is different. I've never let go there[2]—and I never mean to."

The scene left Waythorn deeply shaken[3]. Shamefacedly[4], in indirect ways, he had been finding out about Haskett; and all that he had learned was favorable. The little man, in order to be near his daughter, had sold out his share in a profitable business in Utica, and accepted a modest clerkship[5] in a New York manufacturing house. He boarded[6] in a shabby street[7] and had few acquaintances[8]. His passion for Lily filled his life. Waythorn felt that this exploration of Haskett was like groping about[9] with a dark-lantern in his wife's past; but he saw now that there were recesses[10] his lantern had not explored. He had never inquired into the exact circumstances of his wife's first matrimonial rupture. On the surface all had been fair. It was she who had obtained the divorce, and the court had given her the child. But Waythorn knew how many ambiguities such a verdict might cover[11]. The mere fact that Haskett retained a right over his daughter implied an unsuspected compromise. Waythorn was an idealist. He always refused to recognize unpleasant contingencies till he found himself confronted with them, and then he saw them followed by a special train of consequences. His next

---

1 **to hold on to:** manter; sustentar • 2 **I've never let go there:** nunca renunciei a isso • 3 **deeply shaken:** profundamente abalado • 4 **shamefacedly:** envergonhado • 5 **clerkship:** posto administrativo • 6 **he boarded:** ele se hospedava • 7 **a shabby street:** em uma rua miserável • 8 **had few acquaintances:** tinha poucos conhecidos • 9 **groping about:** tatear; buscar no escuro • 10 **recesses:** recônditos • 11 **cover:** encobrir; ocultar

days were thus haunted¹, and he determined to try to lay the ghosts by conjuring them up² in his wife's presence.

When he repeated Haskett's request a flame of anger passed over her face; but she subdued it³ instantly and spoke with a slight quiver of outraged motherhood⁴.

"It is very ungentlemanly of him," she said.

The word grated on⁵ Waythorn. "That is neither here nor there⁶. It's a bare question of rights."

She murmured: "It's not as if he could ever be a help to Lily⁷—"

Waythorn flushed. This was even less to his taste⁸. "The question is," he repeated, "what authority has he over her?"

She looked downward, twisting herself⁹ a little in her seat. "I am willing¹⁰ to see him—I thought you objected," she faltered¹¹.

In a flash he understood that she knew the extent of Haskett's claims. Perhaps it was not the first time she had resisted them.

"My objecting has nothing to do with it," he said coldly; "if Haskett has a right to be consulted you must consult him."

---

1 **his next days were thus haunted:** seus próximos dias foram consequentemente assombrados • 2 **to try to lay the ghost by conjuring them up:** tentar afugentar os fantasmas, conjurando-os • 3 **she subdued it:** a reprimiu • 4 **a slight quiver of outraged motherhood:** um leve estremecimento de mãe ofendida • 5 **grated on:** irritou • 6 **that is neither here nor there:** isso não vem ao caso • 7 **it's not as if he could ever be a help to Lily:** como se ele pudesse ser de alguma ajuda a Lily • 8 **this was even less to his taste:** isso o agradou ainda menos • 9 **twisting herself:** se remexendo • 10 **I am willing:** estou disposto • 11 **she faltered:** ela balbuciou

She burst into tears, and he saw that she expected him to regard her as a victim.

Haskett did not abuse his rights. Waythorn had felt miserably sure that he would not. But the governess was dismissed[1], and from time to time the little man demanded an interview with Alice. After the first outburst[2] she accepted the situation with her usual adaptability. Haskett had once reminded Waythorn of the piano-tuner, and Mrs. Waythorn, after a month or two, appeared to class him with that domestic familiar[3]. Waythorn could not but respect[4] the father's tenacity. At first he had tried to cultivate the suspicion that Haskett might be "up to" something[5], that he had an object in securing a foothold[6] in the house. But in his heart Waythorn was sure of Haskett's single-mindedness[7]; he even guessed in the latter a mild contempt[8] for such advantages as his relation with the Waythorns might offer. Haskett's sincerity of purpose made him invulnerable, and his successor had to accept him as a lien[9] on the property.

Mr. Sellers was sent to Europe to recover from his gout, and Varick's affairs hung on Waythorn's hands. The negotiations were prolonged and complicated; they necessitated

---

1 **the governess was dismissed:** a governanta foi demitida • 2 **outburst:** explosão • 3 **appeared to class him with that domestic familiar:** parecia incluí-lo na mesma categoria doméstica • 4 **could not but respect:** não poderia senão respeitar • 5 **might be "up to" something:** poderia estar tramando alguma coisa • 6 **securing a foothold:** assegurando um espaço • 7 **single-mindedness:** obstinação • 8 **a mild contempt:** um leve desprezo • 9 **lien:** parte do contrato

frequent conferences between the two men, and the interests of the firm forbade[1] Waythorn's suggesting that his client should transfer his business to another office.

Varick appeared well in the transaction. In moments of relaxation his coarse streak[2] appeared, and Waythorn dreaded[3] his geniality; but in the office he was concise and clear-headed[4], with a flattering[5] deference to Waythorn's judgment. Their business relations being so affably established, it would have been absurd for the two men to ignore each other in society. The first time they met in a drawing-room[6], Varick took up their intercourse in the same easy key[7], and his hostess's[8] grateful glance obliged Waythorn to respond to it. After that they ran across each other frequently, and one evening at a ball Waythorn, wandering through the remoter rooms, came upon[9] Varick seated beside his wife. She colored a little, and faltered in what she was saying; but Varick nodded to Waythorn without rising, and the latter strolled on[10].

In the carriage[11], on the way home, he broke out nervously: "I didn't know you spoke to Varick."

Her voice trembled a little. "It's the first time—he happened to be standing near me; I didn't know what to do.

---

1 **forbade:** proibiam • 2 **his coarse streak:** a sua tendência grosseira; o seu lado rústico • 3 **dreaded:** temia • 4 **clear-headed:** lúcido; inteligente • 5 **flattering:** lisonjeira • 6 **drawing-room:** sala de visitas • 7 **took up their intercourse in the same easy key:** manteve no relacionamento o mesmo trato cordial • 8 **hostess:** anfitriã • 9 **came upon:** deparou com • 10 **strolled on:** continuou caminhando • 11 **carriage:** carruagem

It's so awkward¹, meeting everywhere—and he said you had been very kind about some business."

"That's different," said Waythorn.

She paused a moment. "I'll do just as you wish," she returned pliantly². "I thought it would be less awkward to speak to him when we meet."

Her pliancy was beginning to sicken him³. Had she really no will of her own—no theory about her relation to these men? She had accepted Haskett—did she mean to accept Varick? It was "less awkward," as she had said, and her instinct was to evade difficulties or to circumvent⁴ them. With sudden vividness Waythorn saw how the instinct had developed. She was "as easy as an old shoe"—a shoe that too many feet had worn. Her elasticity was the result of tension in too many different directions. Alice Haskett—Alice Varick—Alice Waythorn—she had been each in turn, and had left hanging to each name a little of her privacy, a little of her personality, a little of the inmost self⁵ where the unknown god abides⁶.

"Yes—it's better to speak to Varick," said Waythorn wearily⁷.

---

1 **awkward:** incômodo • 2 **pliantly:** complacentemente • 3 **to sicken him:** enjoá-lo • 4 **to circumvent them:** contorná-las • 5 **the inmost self:** do mais íntimo do seu ser • 6 **where the unknown god abides:** onde reside o deus desconhecido • 7 **wearily:** de modo cansado; aborrecido

## V

The winter wore on[1], and society took advantage of the Waythorns' acceptance of Varick. Harassed[2] hostesses were grateful to them for bridging over[3] a social difficulty, and Mrs. Waythorn was held up as a miracle of good taste[4]. Some experimental spirits could not resist the diversion of throwing Varick and his former wife together, and there were those who thought he found a zest in[5] the propinquity. But Mrs. Waythorn's conduct remained irreproachable. She neither avoided Varick nor sought him out. Even Waythorn could not but admit that she had discovered the solution of the newest social problem.

He had married her without giving much thought to that problem. He had fancied that a woman can shed[6] her past like a man. But now he saw that Alice was bound to hers[7] both by the circumstances which forced her into continued relation with it, and by the traces it had left on her nature. With grim irony[8] Waythorn compared himself to a member of a syndicate. He held so many shares in his wife's personality and his predecessors were his partners in the business. If there had been any element of passion in the transaction he would have felt less deteriorated by it. The fact that Alice took her change of husbands like a change of weather reduced

---

1 **the winter wore on:** o inverno transcorreu • 2 **harassed:** tensas • 3 **bridging over:** transpor; resolver • 4 **was held up as a miracle of good taste:** tida como um milagre do bom gosto • 5 **he found a zest in:** se deliciava • 6 **shed:** largar; desprender-se • 7 **was bound to hers:** estava presa a seus • 8 **with grim irony:** com uma ironia macabra

the situation to mediocrity. He could have forgiven her for blunders[1], for excesses; for resisting Hackett, for yielding to Varick; for anything but her acquiescence[2] and her tact. She reminded him of a juggler tossing knives[3]; but the knives were blunt[4] and she knew they would never cut her.

And then, gradually, habit formed a protecting surface for his sensibilities. If he paid for each day's comfort with the small change[5] of his illusions, he grew daily to value the comfort more[6] and set less store upon the coin[7]. He had drifted into a dulling propinquity with Haskett and Varick and he took refuge in the cheap revenge of satirizing the situation. He even began to reckon up[8] the advantages which accrued from it[9], to ask himself if it were not better to own a third of a wife who knew how to make a man happy than a whole one who had lacked opportunity to acquire the art. For it was an art, and made up, like all others, of concessions[10], eliminations and embellishments[11]; of lights judiciously thrown and shadows skillfully softened. His wife knew exactly how to manage the lights, and he knew exactly to what training she owed her skill[12]. He even tried to trace the source of his obligations, to discriminate between the influences which had

---

1 **blunders:** erros • 2 **but her acquiescence:** a não ser seu consentimento • 3 **she reminded him of a juggler tossing knives:** ela lhe lembrava um malabarista jogando facas • 4 **blunt:** sem corte; sem fio • 5 **small change:** trocado • 6 **he grew daily to value the comfort more:** a cada dia valorizava mais seu conforto • 7 **set less store upon the coin:** dava menos importância ao dinheiro; estava disposto a pagar o preço • 8 **to reckon up:** reconhecer; avaliar • 9 **which accrued from it:** que advinham dela • 10 **made up ... of concessions:** feito de concessões • 11 **embellishments:** enfeites • 12 **she owed her skill:** ela devia sua habilidade

combined to produce his domestic happiness: he perceived that Haskett's commonness had made Alice worship good breeding[1], while Varick's liberal construction of the marriage bond[2] had taught her[3] to value the conjugal virtues; so that he was directly indebted to his predecessors for the devotion which made his life easy if not inspiring[4].

From this phase he passed into that of complete acceptance. He ceased to satirize himself because time dulled the irony[5] of the situation and the joke lost its humor with its sting[6]. Even the sight of Haskett's hat on the hall table had ceased to touch the springs of epigram[7]. The hat was often seen there now, for it had been decided that it was better for Lily's father to visit her than for the little girl to go to his boarding-house[8]. Waythorn, having acquiesced in[9] this arrangement, had been surprised to find how little difference it made[10]. Haskett was never obtrusive[11], and the few visitors who met him on the stairs were unaware[12] of his identity. Waythorn did not know how often he saw Alice, but with himself Haskett was seldom in contact.

One afternoon, however, he learned on entering that Lily's father was waiting to see him. In the library he found

---

1 **worship good breeding:** venerar o fato de ter bom berço • 2 **the marriage bond:** os laços do matrimônio • 3 **had taught her:** lhe ensinou • 4 **easy if not inspiring:** fácil, senão inspiradora • 5 **time dulled the irony:** o tempo apagou a ironia • 6 **sting:** ferrão • 7 **the springs of epigram:** as molas do epigrama (da ironia) • 8 **boarding-house:** pensão • 9 **having acquiesced in:** tendo consentido • 10 **how little diference it made:** que pouco importava • 11 **was never obtrusive:** nunca se intrometia • 12 **were unaware:** ignoravam

Haskett occupying a chair in his usual provisional way. Waythorn always felt grateful to him for not leaning back[1].

"I hope you'll excuse me, Mr. Waythorn," he said rising. "I wanted to see Mrs. Waythorn about Lily, and your man asked me to wait here till she came in."

"Of course," said Waythorn, remembering that a sudden leak[2] had that morning given over the drawing-room to the plumbers[3].

He opened his cigar-case and held it out[4] to his visitor, and Haskett's acceptance seemed to mark a fresh stage in their intercourse[5]. The spring evening was chilly[6], and Waythorn invited his guest to draw up[7] his chair to the fire. He meant to find an excuse to leave Haskett in a moment; but he was tired and cold, and after all the little man no longer jarred on him[8].

The two were inclosed in the intimacy[9] of their blended cigar-smoke when the door opened and Varick walked into the room. Waythorn rose abruptly. It was the first time that Varick had come to the house, and the surprise of seeing him, combined with the singular inopportuneness of his arrival, gave a new edge[10] to Waythorn's blunted sensibilities[11]. He stared at his visitor without speaking.

Varick seemed too preoccupied to notice his host's embarrassment.

---

1 **leaning back:** reclinar-se; encostar • 2 **leak:** goteira • 3 **plumbers:** encanadores • 4 **held it out:** a ofereceu • 5 **intercourse:** relação • 6 **chilly:** frio • 7 **draw up:** aproximar • 8 **no longer jarred on him:** não o incomodava mais • 9 **inclosed in the intimacy:** fechados na intimidade • 10 **a new edge:** um novo limite • 11 **blunted sensibilities:** sensibilidade anestesiada

"My dear fellow," he exclaimed in his most expansive tone, "I must apologize for tumbling in on you in this way[1], but I was too late to catch you down town, and so I thought—" He stopped short[2], catching sight of Haskett, and his sanguine color deepened to a flush which spread vividly under his scant[3] blond hair. But in a moment he recovered himself and nodded slightly. Haskett returned the bow[4] in silence, and Waythorn was still groping for speech[5] when the footman came in carrying a tea-table.

The intrusion offered a welcome vent[6] to Waythorn's nerves. "What the deuce are you bringing this here for[7]?" he said sharply[8].

"I beg your pardon, sir, but the plumbers are still in the drawing-room, and Mrs. Waythorn said she would have tea in the library." The footman's perfectly respectful tone implied a reflection[9] on Waythorn's reasonableness[10].

"Oh, very well," said the latter resignedly, and the footman proceeded to open the folding[11] tea-table and set out its complicated appointments[12]. While this interminable process continued the three men stood motionless, watching it with a fascinated stare, till Waythorn, to break the silence, said to Varick: "Won't you have a cigar?"

---

1 **tumbling in on you in this way:** aparecer assim sem avisar • 2 **he stopped short:** calou bruscamente • 3 **scant:** escasso • 4 **bow:** saudação • 5 **groping for speech:** tentando falar • 6 **vent:** um respiro • 7 **what the deuce are you bringing this here for?:** por quê, em nome de Deus, você traz isto aqui? • 8 **sharply:** em tom cortante • 9 **reflection:** reflexão • 10 **reasonableness:** sensatez • 11 **folding:** dobrável • 12 **set out the complicated appointments:** dispôs seu equipamento complicado

He held out the case he had just tendered to[1] Haskett, and Varick helped himself[2] with a smile. Waythorn looked about for a match, and finding none, proffered a light[3] from his own cigar. Haskett, in the background, held his ground[4] mildly, examining his cigar-tip now and then, and stepping forward at the right moment to knock its ashes into the fire.

The footman at last withdrew[5], and Varick immediately began: "If I could just say half a word to you about this business—"

"Certainly," stammered Waythorn; "in the dining-room—"

But as he placed his hand on the door it opened from without[6], and his wife appeared on the threshold.

She came in fresh and smiling, in her street dress and hat, shedding a fragrance from the boa which she loosened in advancing[7].

"Shall we have tea in here, dear?" she began; and then she caught sight of Varick. Her smile deepened, veiling[8] a slight tremor of surprise. "Why, how do you do?" she said with a distinct note of pleasure.

As she shook hands with Varick she saw Haskett standing behind him. Her smile faded for a moment, but she recalled it[9] quickly, with a scarcely perceptible side-glance[10] at Waythorn.

---

1 **he had just tendered to:** ele tinha acabado de oferecer • 2 **Varick helped himself:** Varick se serviu • 3 **proffered a light:** ofereceu fogo • 4 **held his ground:** guardou sua distância • 5 **withdrew:** se retirou • 6 **it opened from without:** abriu de fora (forma antiga de falar) • 7 **which she loosened in advancing:** que se soltava enquanto ela caminhava • 8 **veiling:** dissimulando • 9 **she recalled it:** o recuperou • 10 **side-glance:** um olhar de viés

"How do you do, Mr. Haskett?" she said, and shook hands with him a shade[1] less cordially.

The three men stood awkwardly before her, till Varick, always the most self-possessed, dashed into an explanatory phrase[2].

"We—I had to see Waythorn a moment on business," he stammered, brick-red from chin to nape[3].

Haskett stepped forward with his air of mild obstinacy. "I am sorry to intrude; but you appointed five o'clock—" he directed his resigned glance to the time-piece[4] on the mantel.

She swept aside their embarrassment with a charming gesture of hospitality.

"I'm so sorry—I'm always late; but the afternoon was so lovely." She stood drawing her gloves off, propitiatory[5] and graceful, diffusing about her a sense of ease[6] and familiarity in which the situation lost its grotesqueness. "But before talking business," she added brightly, "I'm sure every one wants a cup of tea."

She dropped into her low chair by the tea-table, and the two visitors, as if drawn by her smile[7], advanced to receive the cups she held out.

She glanced about for Waythorn[8], and he took the third cup with a laugh.

---

1 **a shade:** um pouquinho • 2 **dashed into an explanatory phrase :** desatou em uma explicação • 3 **brick-red from chin to nape:** vermelho do queixo até a nuca • 4 **time-piece:** relógio (expressão antiga) • 5 **propitiatory:** conciliadora • 6 **diffusing about her a sense of ease:** irradiando uma sensação de calma • 7 **as if drawn by her smile:** como se atraídos pelo seu sorriso • 8 **she glanced about for Waythorn:** ela procurou Waythorn com o olhar

**1ª edição** fevereiro de 2011 | **Diagramação** Patrícia De Michelis
**Fonte** Bembo e Berthold Akzidenz Grotesk | **Papel** Chamois 75g/m²
**Impressão e acabamento** Yangraf